The
TOWER of ZANID

The
Tower
of
Zanid

by

L. Sprague de Camp

AIRMONT BOOKS
22 EAST 60TH STREET · NEW YORK 22

THE TOWER OF ZANID

An AIRMONT BOOK published by arrangement with
Thomas Bouregy & Company, Inc.

PRINTING HISTORY

Bouregy edition published September, 1958
Airmont edition published February, 1963

©, Copyright, 1958, by L. Sprague de Camp

All rights reserved.

PUBLISHED SIMULTANEOUSLY IN THE DOMINION OF CANADA
BY THE RYERSON PRESS, TORONTO

PRINTED IN THE UNITED STATES OF AMERICA
BY THE COLONIAL PRESS, INC., CLINTON, MASSACHUSETTS

AIRMONT PUBLISHING CO., INC., 22 East 60th St., New York 22, N.Y.

Chapter I

Dr. Julian Fredro got up from the cot, swayed, and steadied himself. The nurse in the dispensary of Novorecife had removed the attachments from him. The lights had stopped flashing and things had stopped going round. Still, he felt a little dizzy. The door opened and Herculeu Castanhoso, the squirrel-like little security officer of the Terran spaceport, came in with a fistful of papers.

"Here you are, Senhor Julian," he said in the Brazilo-Portuguese of the spaceways. "You will find these all in order, but you had better check them to make sure. You have permission to visit Gozashtand, Mikardand, the Free City of Majbur, Qirib, Balhib, Zamba, and all the other friendly Krishnan countries with which we have diplomatic relations."

"Is good," said Fredro.

"I need not caution you about Regulation 368, which forbids you to impart knowledge of Terran science and inventions to natives of H-type planets. The pseudo-hypnosis to which you have just been subjected will effectively prevent your doing so."

"Excuse," said Fredro, speaking Portuguese with a thick Polish accent, "but it seems to me like—what is English expression?—like locking a stable door after cat is out of bag."

Castanhoso shrugged. "What can I do? The leakage occurred before we got artificial pseudo-hypnosis, which was not known until Saint-Remy's work on Osirian telepathic powers a few decades ago. When my predecessor, Abreu, was security officer, I once went out with him to destroy with our own hands a steamship that an Earthman had built for Ferrian, the Pandr of Sotaspe."

"That must have been exciting."

"Exciting is not the word, Senhor Doctor Julian," said Castanhoso with a vigorous gesture. "But the wonder is that the Krishnans did not learn more: guns, for instance, or engines. Of course some claim that they lack the native originality. . . . Speaking of Prince Ferrian, are you going to Sotaspe? He still rules that island—a very vivid personality."

"No," said Fredro. "I go in opposite direction, to Balhib."

"So-yes? I wish you a pleasant journey. It is not bad, now that you can go by bishtar-train all the way to Zanid. What do you hope to accomplish in Balhib, if I may ask?"

Fredro's eyes took on a faraway gleam, as of one who after a hard day's struggle sights a distant bottle of whiskey. "I shall solve the mystery of the Safq."

"You mean that colossal artificial snail-shell?"

"Certainly. To solve the Safq would be a fitting climax to my career. After that I shall retire—I am nearly two hundred—and spend my closing years playing with my great-great-great-great-grandchildren and sneering at work of my younger colleagues. *Obrigado* for your many kindnesses, Senhor Herculeu. I go sightseeing—you stand here like Dutch boy with a thumb in the mouth."

"You mean with his finger in the dyke. It is discouraging," said Castanhoso, "when one sees that the dyke has already broken through in many other places. The technological blockade might have been successful if it had been applied resolutely right at the start, and if we had had the Saint-Remy treatment then. But you, senhor, will see Krishna in flux. It should be interesting."

"That is why I am here. *Ate a vista*, senhor."

It was the festival of 'Anerik, and the fun-loving folk of Zanid were enjoying their holiday on the dusty plain west of the city.

Across the shallow, muddy Eshqa a space of more than a square hoda had been marked off. In one section, lusty young Krishnans were racing shomals and ayas—either riding the beasts or driving them from chariots, sulkies, buggies, and other vehicles. In another, platoons of pikemen paraded to the shout of trumpets and the smash of cymbals while Roqir—the star Tau Ceti—blazed upon their polished helms. Elsewhere, armored jousters nudged each other off their mounts with pronged lances, striking the ground with the clang of a stove dropped from a roof.

On the ball-field, the crowd screamed as Zanid's team of minasht-players beat the diapers off the visiting team from Lussar. King Kir's private band played from a temporary stand that rose amid a sea of booths where you could have your shoes patched, your clothes cleaned, or your hair cut, or buy food, drink, tobacco, jewelry, hats, clothes, walking-sticks, swords, tools, archery equipment, brassware, pottery, medicines (mostly worthless), books, pictures, gods, amulets, potions, seeds, bulbs, lanterns, rugs, furniture, and many other things. Jugglers juggled; acrobats balanced; dancers bounded; actors strutted, and stilt-walkers staggered. Musicians twanged and tootled; singers squalled; poets rhapsodized; story-tellers lied, and fanatics orated. Mountebanks cried up their nostrums; exorcists pursued evil spirits with fireworks; and mothers rushed shrieking after their children.

The celebrants included not only Krishnans but also a sprinkling of folk of other worlds: A pair of Osirians, like small bipedal dinosaurs with their scaly bodies painted in intricate patterns, dashing excitedly from one sight to another; a trio of furry, beady-eyed Thothians, half the height of the Krishnans, trimming the natives at the gambling-games of a dozen worlds; a centaur-like Vishnuvan morosely munching greens from a big leather bag. There was a sober Ormazdian couple, near-human and crested, their carmine skins bare but for sandals and skimpy mantles hanging down their backs; and, of course, a group of trousered Terran tourists with their women, and their cameras in little leather cases.

Here and there you could see an Earthman who had gone Krishnan, swathed from waist to knee in the dhoti-like loin-garment of the land, and wearing a native stocking-cap with its end wound turbanwise about his head. A few decades before, they would all have disguised themselves by dyeing their hair blue-green, wearing large pointed artificial ears, and gluing to their foreheads a pair of feathery antennae, in imitation of the Krishnans' external organs of smell. These organs were something like extra eyebrows rising from the inner ends of the true eyebrows.

One particular Earthman sauntered about the grounds near the bandstand as if he had nothing on his mind. He wore the usual oversized diaper and a loose striped shirt or tunic wherein several holes had been neatly mended; a plain Krishnan rapier swung at his hip. He was tall for an Earthman—about the average height of a Krishnan, who, through Earthly eyes, seemed a tallish, lean race of humanoids with olive-greenish complexions and flat features like those of the Terran Mongoloid race.

This man, however, was of the white race, with the fair coloring of the Northwestern European, though his uncovered hair, worn nape-length in Balhibo style, was graying at the sides. In his younger days, he had been outstandingly handsome, with an aggressively aquiline nose; now the bags under the bloodshot eyes and the network of little red veins spoiled the initial impression. If he had never taken the longevity doses with which Terrans tripled their life-span, one would have guessed him to be in his early forties. Actually he was ninety-four Terran years of age.

This man was Anthony Fallon, of London, Great Britain, Earth. For a little while, he had been king of the isle of Zamba in Krishna's Sadabao Sea. Unfortunately, in an excess of ambition, he had attacked the mighty Empire of Gozashtand with a trainload of followers and two dozen smuggled machine-guns. In so doing he had brought down upon his head the wrath of the Interplanetary Council. The I. C. sought to enforce a technological blockade on Krishna, to keep the warlike but pre-industrial natives of that charming planet from learning the more destructive methods of scientific warfare until they had advanced far enough in politics and culture to make such a revelation safe. Under these circumstances, of course, a crate of machine-guns was strictly tabu.

As a result Fallon had been snatched from his throne and imprisoned in Gozashtand under a cataleptic trance. This continued for many years, until his second wife, Julnar—who had been forced to return to Earth—came back to Krishna and effected his release. Fallon, free, had tried to regain his throne, failed, had lost Julnar, and now lived in Zanid, the capital of Balhib.

Fallon wandered past the prefect's pavilion, from the central pole of which flowed the green-and-black flag of Kir, the Dour of Balhib, straining stiffly in the brisk breeze from the steppes. Below it flapped the special flag of this festival, bearing the dragon-like shan from the equatorial forests of Mutaabwk, on which the demigod 'Anerik was supposed to have ridden into Balhib to spread enlightenment thousands of years ago. Then Fallon headed through the tangle of booths toward the bandstand, whence wafted faintly the strains of a march which a Terran named Schubert had composed over three centuries before.

Schubert was hard put to it to make himself heard over a loud voice with a strange Terran accent. Fallon tracked the orator down and found another Earthman speaking wretched Balhibou with impassioned gestures from atop a box:

". . . beware the wrath of the one God! For this God hates iniquity—especially the sins of idolatry, frivolity, and immodesty, to all of which you Balhibuma are subject. Let me save you from the wrath to come! Repent before it is too late! Destroy the temples of the false gods! . . ."

Fallon listened briefly. The speaker was a burly fellow in a black Terran suit, his nondescript face taut with the tensions of fanaticism, and long black hair escaping from under a snowy turban. He seemed particularly wrought up over the female national dress of Balhib, consisting of a pleated skirt and a shawl pinned about the shoulders. Fallon recognized the doctrines of the Ecumenical Monotheists, a widespread syncretic sect of Brazilian origin that had gotten its start after World War III on Earth. The Krishnan audience seemed more amused than impressed.

When tired of repetition, Fallon moved along with a more

purposeful air. He was halted by a triumphal procession from the minasht-field, as the partisans of Zanid bore the captain of the local team past upon their shoulders, with his broken arm in a sling. When the sports enthusiasts had gotten out of the way, Fallon walked past a shooting-gallery where Krishnans twanged light crossbows at targets, and stopped before a tent with a sign in Balhibou reading:

TURANJ THE SEER

Astrologer, scryer, necromancer, odontomancer. Sees all, knows all, tells all. Futures foretold; opportunities revealed; dooms averted; lost articles found; courtships planned; enemies exposed. Let me help you!

Fallon put his head into the door of the tent, a large one divided into compartments. In the vestibule a wrinkled Krishnan sat on a hassock smoking a long cigar.

Fallon said in fluent Balhibou: "Hello, Qais old man. What have you committed lately?"

"In Balhib I'm Turanj," replied the Krishnan sharply. "Forget it not, sir!"

"Turanj then. May I enter, O seer?"

The Krishnan flicked an ash. "Indeed you may, my son. Wherefore would you rend the veil?"

Fallon let fall the flap behind him. "You know, sagacious one. If you'll lead the way . . ."

Turanj grunted, arose, and led Fallon into the main compartment of the tent, where a table stood between two hassocks. Each took a hassock, and Turanj (or Qais of Babaal as he was known in his native Qaath) said: "Well, Antane my chick, what's of interest this time?"

"Let's see some cash first."

"You're as niggardly with your facts as Dakhaq with his gold." Qais produced a bag of coins from nowhere and set it down upon the table with a clink. He untied the draw-string and fingered out a couple of golden ten-kard pieces.

"Proceed."

Fallon thought, then said: "Kir's worse. He took offense at the beard worn by the envoy of the Republic of Katai-Jhogorai. Compared to Terran whiskers, you could hardly see this beard—but the king ordered the envoy's head off. Embarrassing, what? Especially to the poor envoy. It was all Chabarian could do to hustle the fellow out and send him packing, meanwhile assuring the Dour that the victim had been dispatched. Of course, he had been—but in another sense."

Qais chuckled. "Right glad am I that I'm no minister to a

king madder than Gedik, who tried to lasso the moons. Why's Kir so tetchy on the theme of whiskers?"

"Oh, don't you know that story? He once grew one himself—twelve or fourteen whole hairs' worth—and then the Grand Master of the Order of Qarar in Mikardand sent one of his knights on a quest to bag this same beard. It seems that this knight had done in some local bloke, and Kir had been giving Mikardand trouble, so Juvain figured on giving 'em both a lesson. Well, Sir Shurgez got the beard, and that pushed Kir off the deep end. He'd already been acting eccentric—now he went completely balmy, and has remained in that interesting state ever since."

Qais passed over the two golden coins. "One for the news of Kir's madness, and the other for the tale wherewith you embellished it. The Kamuran will relish it. But proceed."

Fallon thought again. "There's a plot against Kir."

"There always is."

"This looks like the real thing. There's a chap named Chindor—Chindor er-Qinan, a nephew of one of the rebellious nobles liquidated by Kir when he abolished feudal tenure. He's out to grab the throne from Kir, as *he* claims, from the highest motives."

"They always do," murmured Qais.

Fallon shrugged. "He might have pure motives at that, who knows? I once knew an honest man. Anyway, Chindor's backed by one of our new middle-class magnates, Liyara the Brassfounder, the story being that Chindor's promised Liyara a protective tariff against brasswork from Madhiq in return for his support."

"Another Terran improvement," said Qais. "If the idea spreads much farther, 'twill utterly ruin this planet's trade. What details?"

"None beyond what I've told you. If you make it worth my while I'll dig into it. The more worth, the more dig."

Qais handed over another coin. "Dig, and then shall we decide how much 'tis worth. Aught else?"

"There's some trouble caused by Terran missionaries—Cosmotheists and Monotheists, and the like. The native medicinemen have been stirring up their flocks against them. Chabarian tries to protect 'em because he's afraid of Novorecife."

Qais grinned. "The more troubles of this sort, the better for us. What else have you?"

Fallon held out his hand palm up and twiddled the fingers. Qais said: "For small news like that, which I knew already, smaller pay."

He dropped a five-kard piece into the palm. Fallon scowled. "O sage, were that disguise never so perfect, yet should I know you by your lack of generosity."

He put away the coin and continued: "The priests of Bakh are campaigning against the cult of Yesht again. The Bakhites accuse the Yeshtites of human sacrifices and such abominations, and claim it's an outrage that they—the state religion—may not extirpate the worship of the god of darkness. They hope to catch Kir in one of his madder moods and get him to revoke the contract made by his uncle Balade giving the Yeshtites perpetual use of the Safq."

"Hmm," said Qais, handing over another ten-kard piece. "Aught else?"

"Not this time."

"Who built this Safq?"

Fallon performed the Krishnan equivalent of a shrug. "The gods know! I suppose I could dig out more details in the library."

"Have you ever been in the structure?"

"How much of a fool do you take me for? One doesn't stick one's head into the pile unless one's a confirmed Yeshtite—that is, if one wishes to keep one's head."

"Rumors have come to us of strange things taking place in the Safq," said Qais.

"You mean the Yeshtites are doing as the Bakhites say?"

"Nay, these rumors deal not with matters sacerdotal. What the Yeshtites do I know not. But 'tis said that within that sinister structure, men—if they indeed be such—devise means to the scath and hurt of the Empire of Qaath."

Fallon shrugged again.

"Well, if you'd truly make your fortune, find out! 'Tis worth a thousand karda, a true and complete report upon the Safq. And tell me not you'll ne'er consider it. You'd do anything for gold enough."

"Not for a million karda," said Fallon.

"By the green eyes of Hoi, you shall! The Kamuran insists."

Fallon made an impractical suggestion as to what the mighty Ghuur of Uriiq, Kamuran of Qaath, might do with his money.

"Harken," wheedled Qais. "A thousand'll buy you blades enough to set you back upon the throne of Zamba! Does that tempt you not?"

"Not in the least. A moldy cadaver doesn't care whether it's on a throne or not."

"Be not that the goal for which for many years you've striven, like Qarar moiling at his nine labors?"

"Yes, but hope deferred maketh one skeptical. I wouldn't

even consider such a project unless I knew in advance what I was getting into—say if I had a plan of the building, and a schedule of the activities in it."

"If I had all that, I'd have no need to hire a Terran creature to snoop for me." Qais spat upon the floor in annoyance. "You've taken grimmer chances. You Earthmen baffle me betimes. Perchance I could raise the offer by a little . . ."

"To Hishkak with it," snapped Fallon, rising. "How shall I get in touch with you next time?"

"I remain in Zanid for a day or twain. Come to see me at Tashin's Inn."

"Where the players and mountebanks stay?"

"For sure—do I not play the part of such a one?"

"You do it so naturally, maestro!"

"Hmph! But none knows who I really be, so guard your saucy tongue. Farewell!"

Fallon said good-bye and sauntered out into the bright sunshine of Roqir. He mentally added his takings: forty-five karda—enough to support him and Gazi for a few ten-nights. But it was hardly enough to start him on the road back to his throne.

Fallon knew his own weakness well enough to know that if he ever did make the killing for which he hoped, he would have to set about hiring his mercenaries and regaining his throne quickly, for he was one through whose fingers money ran like water. He would dearly love the thousand karda of which Qais had spoken, but asking him to invade the Safq was just too much. Others had tried it and had always come to mysterious ends.

He stopped at a drink-shop and bought a bottle of kvad, Krishna's strongest liquor, something like diluted vodka as to taste. Like most Earthmen on Krishna, he preferred the plain stuff to the highly spiced varieties favored by most Krishnans. The taste mattered little to him; he drank to forget his disappointments.

"Oh, Fallon!" said a sharp, incisive voice.

Fallon turned. His first fear was justified. Behind him stood another Earthman: tall, lean, black-skinned, and frizz-haired. Instead of a Balhibo diaper, he wore a fresh Terran suit. In every way but stature he posed a sharp contrast to Fallon with his crisp voice, his precise gestures, and his alert manner. He bore the air of a natural leader fully aware of his own superiority. He was Percy Mjipa, consul for the Terran World Federation at Zanid.

Fallon composed his features into a noncommittal blank. For a number of reasons, he did not like Percy Mjipa and could not bend himself to smile hypocritically at the consul. He said: "Hello, Mr. Mjipa."

"What are you doing today?" Mjipa spoke English fluently but with the staccato, resonant accent of the cultured Bantu.

"Eating a lotus, old man—just eating a lotus."

"Would you mind stepping over to the prefectural pavilion with me? There's a man I should like you to meet."

Mystified, Fallon followed Mjipa. He knew perfectly well that he was not the sort of person whom Mjipa would exhibit with pride to a visiting dignitary as an example of an Earthman making good on Krishna.

They passed the drill-field, where a company of the Civic Guard of Zanid was parading: platoons of pikemen and arbalestiers. These were a little ragged in their marching, lacking the polish of Kir's professionals; but they made a brave showing in their scarlet tunics under shirts of blackened ring-mail.

Mjipa looked narrowly at Fallon. "I thought you were in the Guard too?"

"I am. In fact, I'm on patrol tonight. With cat-like tread . . ."

"Then why aren't you out there parading?"

Fallon grinned. "I'm in the Juru Company, which is about half non-Krishnans. Can't you imagine Krishnans, Terrans, Osirians, Thothians, and the rest all lined up for a parade?"

"The thought is a bit staggering—something out of a delerium tremens or a TV horror-show."

"And what would you do with our eight-legged Isidian?"

"I suppose you could let him carry a guidon," said Mjipa, and passed on. They came within range of the Terran missionary, who was still ranting.

"Who's he?" asked Fallon. "He seems to hate everything."

"His name is Wagner—Welcome Wagner. American, I believe, and an Ecumenical Monotheist."

"America's gift to interplanetary misunderstanding, eh?"

"You might say so. The odd thing is, he's a reformed adventurer. His name is really Daniel Wagner; as Dismal Dan he was notorious around the Cetic planets as a worse swindler than Borel and Koshay put together. A man of no culture."

"What happened to him? Get thrown in pokey?"

"Exactly, and got religion—as the Americans say—while brooding on his sins in the Novorecife jail. As soon as he got out, the E. M.'s, having no missionaries in the West, signed him on. But now he's a bigger nuisance than ever." A worried shadow flickered across the dark face. "Those fellows give me a worse headache than simple crooks like you."

"Crooks like me? My dear Percy, you wound me, and what's

more you wrong me. I've never in my life . . ."

"Oh, come on, come on. I know all about you. Or at least," corrected the meticulous Mjipa, "more than you think I do."

They came to the big banner-decked tent. The African crisply acknowledged the salutes of the halberdiers who guarded the entrance to the pavilion, and strode in. Fallon followed him through a tangle of passages to a room that had been set aside for the consul's use during the festival. There sat a stocky, squarish, wrinkled man with bristling, short-cut white hair, a snub nose, wide cheek-bones, innocent-looking blue eyes, and a white mustache and goatee. He was carelessly dressed in Terran travelling-clothes. As they entered, this man stood up and took his pipe out of his mouth.

"Dr. Fredro," said Mjipa, "here's your man. His name is Anthony Fallon. Fallon, this is Dr. Julian Fredro."

"Thank you," Fredro murmured in acknowledgment, head slightly bowed and eyes shifting, as if with embarrassment or shyness.

Mjipa continued: "Dr. Fredro's here for some archeological research, and while he's about it, he's taking in all the sights. He is the most indefatigable sight-seer I've yet experienced."

Fredro made a self-deprecating motion, saying in Slavic-accented English: "Mr. Mjipa exaggerates, Mr. Fallon. I find Krishna interesting place, that's all. So I try to make hay while cat is away."

"He's run my legs off," sighed Mjipa.

"Oh, not really," said Fredro. "I like to learn language of countries I visit, and mix with people. I am studying the language now. As for people—ah—Mr. Fallon, do you know any Balhibo philosophers in Zanid? Mr. Mjipa has introduced me to soldiers, noblemen, merchants, and workers, but no intellectuals."

"I'm afraid not," said Fallon. "The Krishnans don't go in much for exploring the country of the mind, especially the Balhibuma, who consider 'emselves a martial race and all that sort of thing. The only philosopher I ever knew was Sainian bad-Sabzovan, some years ago at the court of the Dour of Gozashtand. And I never could understand him."

"Where is this philosopher now?"

Fallon shrugged. "Where are the snows of yesteryear?"

Mjipa said: "Well, I'm sure you can still show Dr. Fredro a lot of things of interest. There is one thing he's particularly anxious to see, which ordinary tourists never do."

"What's that?" asked Fallon. "If you mean Madame Farudi's place in the Izandu . . ."

"No, no, nothing like that. He merely wants you to get him into the Safq."

Chapter II

Fallon stared, then cried, "What?"

"I said," repeated Mjipa, "that Dr. Fredro wants you to get him into the Safq. You know what that is, don't you?"

"Certainly. But what in the name of Bakh does he want to do that for?"

"If—if I may explain," said Fredro. "I am archeologist."

"One of those blokes who digs up a piece of broken butter-plate and reconstructs the history of the Kalwm Empire from it? Go on—I rumble to you."

The visitor made motions with his hands, but seemed to have trouble getting the words out. "Look, Mr. Fallon. Visualize. You know Krishna is great experiment."

"Yes?"

"Interplanetary Council tries to protect the people of this planet against too-fast cultural change by their technological blockade. Of course that has not worked altogether. Some Earthly inventions and—ah—customs leaked through before they gave visitors pseudo-hypnotic treatment, and others like the printing press have been allowed to come in. So today we see—how shall I say?—we witness native cultures beginning to crumble under impact of Terran cultural radiation. Is important that all information about native culture and history be got quickly, before this process runs its course."

"Why?"

"Because first effect of such cultural change is—is to destroy the veneration of affected population for native traditions, history, monuments, relics—everything of that kind. But takes much longer to—ah—to inculcate in them the intellectual regard for such things characteristic of—of well-developed industrio-scientific culture."

Fallon fidgeted impatiently. Between the polysyllabic abstractions and the thick accent, he was not sure that he understood half of what Fredro was saying.

Fredro continued: "As example, one nineteenth-century pasha of Egypt planned to tear down Great Pyramid of Khufu for building-stone, under impression he was being enlightened modern statesman, like commercial-minded Europeans he knew."

"Yes, yes, yes, but what's that got to do with our sticking our heads into a noose by breaking into that thing? I know there's a cult based upon alleged measurements of the interior . . . What's that gang, Percy?"

"The Neophilosophical Society," said Mjipa, "or as the Krishnan branch calls itself, the Mejraf Janjira."

"What is?" asked Fredro.

"Oh, they believe that every planet has some monument—like that Egyptian pyramid you mentioned, or the Tower of the Gods on Ormazd—by whose measurements you can prophesy the future history of the planet. Their idea is that these things were put up by some space-travelling race, before the beginning of recorded history, who knew all future history because they'd seen it by means of a time-travelling gadget. Naturally they picked the Safq for that honor on Krishna. They turn people like that loose here, and then wonder why Krishnans consider all Earthmen cracked."

Fallon said: "Well, I'm no scientist, Dr. Fredro, but I hardly suppose you take that sort of thing seriously. I must say you don't look cracked, at least not on the outside."

"Certainly not," said Fredro.

"Then why are you so anxious to get inside? You won't find anything but a lot of stone passageways and rooms, some fitted up for the Yeshtite services."

"You see, Mr. Fallon," said Fredro, "no other Terran has ever got into it and it might—ah—fling light on the history of the Kalwm and pre-Kalwm periods. If nobody goes in, then Balhibuma might destroy it when their own culture breaks down."

"All very well, old chap. Not that I have any objection to science, mind you. Wonderful thing and all that."

"Thank you," said Fredro.

"But if you want to risk your neck, you'll have to do it on your own."

"But, Mr. Fallon . . ."

"Not interested. Definitely, absolutely, positively."

"You would not—ah—be asked to contribute your services for gratis, you know. I have a small allowance on my appropriation for employ of native assistance . . ."

"You forget," broke in Mjipa, with an edge in his voice, "that Mr. Fallon, despite his manner of life, is not a Krishnan."

Fredro waved a placatory hand, stammering: "I m-meant no slight, gentlemen . . ."

"Oh, stow it," said Fallon. "I'm not insulted. I don't share Percy's prejudices against Krishnans."

"I am not prejudiced," protested Mjipa. "Some of my best friends are Krishnans. But another species is another species, and one should always bear it in mind."

"Meaning they're all right so long as they keep their place," said Fallon, grinning wickedly.

"Not how I should have expressed it, but it's the general idea."

"Yes?"

"Yes. Different races of one species may be substantially the same mentally, as among Terrans—but different species are something else."

"But we are talking about Krishnans," said Fredro. "And psychological tests show no differences in average intelligence-level. Or if there are differences of averages, overlap is so great that average-differences are negligible."

"You may trust your tests," said Mjipa, "but I've known these beggars personally for years, and you can't tell me they display human inventiveness and originality."

Fallon spoke up: "But look here, how about the inventions they've made? They've developed a crude camera of their own, for instance. When did *you* invent something, Percy?"

Mjipa made an impatient gesture. "All copied from Terran examples. Leaks in the blockade."

"No," said Fredro. "Is not it either. Krishnan camera is case of—ah—stimulus-diffusion."

"What?" said Mjipa.

"Stimulus-diffusion, term invented by American anthropologist Kroeber, about two centuries ago."

"What does it mean?" asked Mjipa.

"Where they hear of something in use elsewhere and develop their own version without have seen it. Some primitive Terrans a few centuries ago developed writing that way. But it still requires inventiveness."

Mjipa persisted: "Well, even granting all you claim, these natives do differ temperamentally from us, and intelligence does no good without the will to use it."

"How do you know they are different?" asked Fredro.

"There was some psychologist who tested a lot of them and pointed out that they lack some of our Terran forms of insanity altogether, such as paranoia . . ."

Fallon broke in: "Isn't paranoia what that loon Kir's got?"

Mjipa shrugged. "Not my field. But that's what this chap said, also pointing out their strong tendency toward hysteria and sadism."

Fredro persisted: "That is not what I had so much in the mind. I have not been here before, but I have studied Krishnan arts and crafts on Earth, and these show the highest degree of imaginative fertility—sculpture, poetry, and such . . ."

Fallon, stifling a yawn, interrupted: "Mind saving the debate till I've gone? I don't understand half of what you're talking about. . . . Now, how much would this stipend be?" he asked, more from curiosity than from any intention of seriously considering the offer.

"Two and one-half karda a day," replied Fredro.

While this was a high wage in Balhib, Fallon had just turned down a lump-sum offer of a thousand. "Sorry, Dr. Fredro. No sale."

"Possibly I could—I could squeeze a little more out of . . ."

"No sir! Not for ten times that offer. People have tried to get into that thing before and always came to a bad end."

"Well," said Mjipa, "you're destined for a bad end sooner or later anyway."

"I still prefer it later rather than sooner. As you gentlemen know, I'll take a chance—but that's not a chance, it's a certainty."

"Look here," said Mjipa. "I promised Dr. Fredro assistance, and you owe me for past favors, and I particularly wish you to take the job."

Fallon shot a sharp look at the consul. "Why particularly?"

Mjipa said: "Dr. Fredro, will you excuse us a few minutes? Wait here for me. Come along, Fallon."

"Thank you," said Fredro.

Fallon, scowling, followed Mjipa outside. When they found a place with nobody near, Mjipa said in a low voice: "Here's the story. Three Earthmen have disappeared from my jurisdiction in the past three years, and I haven't found a trace of them. And they're not the sort of men who'd normally get into bad company and get their throats cut."

"Well?" said Fallon. "If they were trying to get into the Safq, that proves my point. Serves them right."

"I have no reason to believe they were *trying* to enter the Safq—but they might have been taken into it. In any case, I should be remiss in my duty, when confronted with a mystery like this, if I didn't exhaust all efforts to solve it."

Fallon shook his head. "If you want to get into that monstrosity, go ahead . . ."

"If it weren't for the color of my skin, which can't be disguised, I would." Mjipa gripped Fallon's arm. "So you, my dear Fallon, are going in, and don't think you're not."

"Why? To make a fourth at bridge with these missing blighters?"

"To find out what happened. Good God, man, would you leave a fellow-Terran to the mercies of these savages?"

"That would depend. Some Terrans, yes."

"But one of your own kind . . ."

"I," said Fallon, "try to judge people on their individual merits, whether they have arms or trunks or tentacles, and I think that's a lot more civilized attitude than yours."

"Well, I suppose there's no use appealing to your patriotism, then. But if you come around next ten-night for your longevity-dose, don't be surprised if I'm just out of them."

"I can get them on the black market if I have to."

Mjipa glared at Fallon with deadly fixity. "And how long d'you think you'd live to enjoy your longevity if I told Chabarian about your spying for the Kamuran of Qaath?"

"My sp— I don't know what you're talking about," replied Fallon, icy fear shooting down his spine.

"Oh, yes you do. And don't think I wouldn't tell him."

"So . . . with all your noble talk, you'd betray a fellow-Terran to the Krishnans after all?"

"I don't like to, but you leave me no other choice. You're no asset to the human race as you are—lowering our prestige in the eyes of the natives."

"Then why bother with me?"

"Because, with all your faults, you're just the man for a job like this, and I won't hesitate to force you to it."

"How could I get in without a disguise?"

"I'll furnish that. Now, I'm going back into that pavilion, either to tell Fredro you'll make the arrangements, or to tell Kir's minister about your meetings with that snake, Qais of Babaal. Which shall it be?"

Fallon turned his bloodshot eyes upon the consul. "Can you furnish me with some advance information? A plan of the interior, for instance, or a libretto of the rites of Yesht?"

"No. I believe the Neophilosophers know, or think they know, something about the interior of the building—but I don't know of any members of that cult in Balhib. You'll have to dig that stuff up yourself. Well?"

Fallon paused a minute more. Then, seeing Mjipa about to speak again, he said: "Oh, hell. You win, damn you. Now, let's have some data. Who are these three missing Earthmen?"

"Well, there was Lavrenti Botkin, the popular-science writer. He went out to walk on the city wall one evening and never came back."

"I read something about it in the *Rashm* at the time. Go on."

"And there was Candido Soares, a Brazilian engineer—and Adam Daly, an American factory manager."

Fallon asked, "Do you notice anything about their occupations?"

"They're all technical people, in one sense or another."

"Mightn't somebody be trying to round up scientists and

engineers to build modern weapons for them? That sort of thing has been tried, you know."

"I thought of that. If I remember rightly," said Mjipa, "you once attempted something of the sort yourself."

"Now, now, Percy, let's let the dead past bury the dead."

Mjipa continued: "But that was before we had the Saint-Remy pseudo-hypnotic treatment. If only it had been developed a few decades earlier . . . Anyway, these people couldn't give out such knowledge—even under torture—any more than you or I could. The natives know that. However, when we find these missing people, we shall no doubt find the reason for their abduction."

Chapter III

The Long Krishnan day died. As he opened his own front door, Anthony Fallon's manner acquired a subtle furtiveness. He slipped stealthily in, quietly took off his sword-belt, and hung it on the hatrack.

He stood for a moment, listening, then tiptoed into the main room. From a shelf he took down a couple of small goblets of natural crystal, the product of the skilled fingers of the artisans of Majbur. They were practically the only items of value in the shabby little living-dining room. Fallon had picked them up during one of his rare flush periods.

Fallon uncorked the bottle (the Krishnans had not yet achieved the felicity of screw-caps) and poured two hookers of kvad. At the gurgle of the liquid a female Krishnan voice spoke from the kitchen: "Antane?"

"It is I, dear," said Fallon in Balhibou. "Home the hero . . ."

"So there you are! I hope you enjoyed your worthless self at the Festival. By 'Anerik the Enlightener, I might be a slave for all the entertainment I receive."

"Now, Gazi my love, I've told you time and again . . ."

"Of course you've told me! But need I believe such moonshine? How big a fool think you I am? Why I ever accepted you as *jagain* I know not."

Stung to his own defense, Fallon snapped: "Because you were a brotherless woman, without a home of your own. Now stop yammering and come in and have a drink. I've got something to show you."

"You *zaft!*" began the woman furiously, then as the import of his words sank in: "Oh, in that case, I'll come forthwith."

The curtain to the kitchen parted and Fallon's jagaini entered. She was a tall, powerfully built Krishnan woman, well made and attractive by Krishnan standards. Her relationship to Fallon was neither that of mistress nor that of wife, but something of both.

For the Balhibuma did not recognize marriage, holding it impractical in a warrior race, such as they had been in earlier centuries. Instead each woman lived with one of her brothers, and was visited at intervals by her jagain—a voluntary relationship terminable at whim, but exclusive while it lasted. Meanwhile the brother reared the children. Therefore, instead of the patronymics of the other Varasto nations, the Balhibuma tagged themselves with the name of the maternal uncle who had reared them. Gazi's full name was Gazi er-Doukh, Gazi the niece of Doukh. A woman who—like Gazi—actually lived with her jagain was deemed unfortunate and déclassé.

Fallon, looking at Gazi in the doorway, wondered if he had been so clever in choosing Krishna as the scene of his extraterrestrial activities. Why didn't he walk out on her? She could not stop him. But she cooked well; he was fond of her in a way . . .

Fallon held up the goblet that he had poured for her. She took it, saying: " 'Tis grateful, but I ween you've spent the last of our housekeeping money on it."

Fallon dug out the wallet that hung from his belt, and displayed the fistful of gold pieces that he had extracted from Qais. Gazi's eyes widened; her hand shot out to snatch. Fallon jerked the money back, laughing, then handed her two tenkard coins. The rest he put back in the wallet.

"That should keep the menage running for a few ten-nights," he said. "When you need more, ask."

"*Bakhan*," she muttered, sinking into the other chair and sipping. "If I know you, 'twill do no good to ask where you got these."

"None whatever," he replied cheerfully. "Some day you'll learn that I *never* discuss business. That's one reason I'm alive."

"A vile, indign business, I'll warrant."

"It feeds us. What's dinner?"

"Cutlets of unha with badr, and a tunest for dessert. Is your mysterious business over for the day?"

"I think so," he responded cautiously.

"Then what hinders you from taking me to the Festival this eve? There'll be fireworks and a mock battle."

"Sorry, dear, but you forget I've got the guard tonight."

"Always something!" She stared gloomily at her glass. "What have I done to the gods that they should hold me in such despite?"

"Have another drink and you'll feel better. Some day, when

I get my throne back . . ."

"How long have I heard that same song?"

". . . when I get my throne back, there'll be fun and games enough. Meanwhile, business before pleasure."

The third section of the Juru Company of the Civic Guard, or Municipal Watch, of Zanid was already falling in when Fallon arrived at the armory. He snatched his bill from the rack and stepped into his place.

As Fallon had explained to Mjipa at the Festival, it was impractical to exhibit the Juru Company on parade. The Juru district was largely inhabited by poor non-Krishnans, and its representation in the Watch resembled a sampling of all the Earth-type planets having intelligent inhabitants. Besides the Krishnans, there were several other Earthmen: Weems, Kisari, Nunez, Ramanand, and so on. There were twelve Osirians and thirteen Thothians. There was a Thorian (not to be confused with the Thothians)—something like an ostrich with arms instead of wings. There was an Isidian—an eight-legged nightmare combination of elephant and dachshund. And others of still different form and origin.

In front of the line of guards stood the well-made Captain Kordaq er-Gilan, of the regular army of Balhib, frowning from under the towering crest of his helmet. Fallon knew why Kordaq glowered. The captain was a conscientious spit-and-polish soldier, who would have loved to beat a company of civic guards into machine-like precision and uniformity. But what sort of uniformity could one expect from such a heterogeneous crew? It was useless even to try to make them buy uniforms; the Thothians claimed that clothes over their fur would stifle them, and no tailor in Balhib would have undertaken to cut a suit for the Isidian.

"*Zuho'i!*" cried Captain Kordaq, and the jagged line came to some sort of attention.

The captain announced: "There shall be combat drill for all my heroes upon the western plain next Fiveday, during the hour after Roqir's red rays first shed their carmine beams upon it. We shall bring . . ."

Captain Kordaq exhibited to an extreme degree the Krishnan tendency to wrap his speech, even the simplest sentences, in fustian magniloquence. At this point, however, he was interrupted by a long loud chorus of groans from the section.

"Wherefore in Hishkak do you resty knaves waul like the creak of an aged tree in a gale?" cried the captain. "One would surmise from these ululations that you'd been commanded on pain of evisceration to slay a shan with a dust-broom!"

"Combat drill!" moaned Savaich, the fat tavernkeeper from Shimad Street, and the senior squad-leader of the section. "Of what use would that be to us? Well ye know one mounted Junga could scatter the whole company with a few flights of arrows, as Qarar scattered the hosts of Dupulan. Then why this silly soldier-playing?"

Junga was the Balhibo term for one of the steppe-dwellers to the west: the fierce folk of Qaath, Dhaukia, or Yeramis.

Kordaq said: "For shame, Master Savaich, that one of our martial race should speak so cowardly! 'Tis the express command of the minister that all companies of the Civic Guard do exercise at arms, willy-nilly."

"I'll resign," muttered Savaich.

"Resignations are not being accepted, poltroon!" Kordaq lowered his voice confidently. "Betwixt me and ye, a vagrant rumor has been wafted by the breeze from the steppes to my ears, saying: the state of the West is indeed parlous and threatening. The Kamuran of Qaath—may Yesht make his eyes fall out—has called up his tribal levies and is marching to and fro throughout the length and breadth of his whole immense domain." He pronounced "Qaath" something like "Qasf," for the Balhibo tongue has no dentals.

"He cannot so assail us!" said Savaich. "We've done nought to provoke him, and besides he swore not to in the treaty that followed the Battle of Tajrosh."

Kordaq gave an exaggerated sigh. "So, old tun of lard, thought the good folk of Jo'ol and Suria and Dhaukia and other places I could mention, had I nothing else to do this night save bandy arguments. At any event, such are your orders. Now off upon your rounds, and let not the reek of the wine-shop, nor the enticements of the giglot, seduce you from the speedy execution of your allotted task. Watch well for thieves who rape from citizens' doorways their very good-gongs. There's come a veritable plague of such thefts since preparations for sanguinary strife have driven up the price of metal.

"Now, then, Master Antane, take your squad to the eastern metes of the district via Ya'fal Street, circling the Safq and returning via Barfur Street. Take particular notice of the alleys near the fountain of Qarar. There have been three robberies and a dolorous murder there during the last ten-night: a reeky disgrace to the virtuous vigilance of the Guard. Master Mokku, you shall patrol . . ."

As each squad received its orders, it broke ranks and wandered off into the night, bills at all angles and bodies swathed against the cold in thick quilted over-tunics. For while the seasons are less pronounced on Krishna than on Earth, the diurnal temperature range is considerable, especially in a prairie region like that in which Zanid stands.

Fallon's squad comprised three persons besides himself: two Krishnans and an Osirian. It was unusual for non-Krishnans to hold offices of command, but the polyethnic Juru Company made its own rules.

To be sent to cover the district wherein lay the Safq suited Fallon fine. The squad cut through an alley on to Ya'fal Street and proceeded along that thoroughfare—two on each side— peering into doorways for signs of burglary or other irregularities. The two largest of Krishna's three moons, Karrim and Golnaz, provided an illumination which, though wan, was adequate when supplemented by the light of the little fires burning in iron cressets at the main intersections. Once the squad passed the cart, drawn by a single shaihan, that made the rounds of the city every night replenishing the fuel in these holders.

Fallon had heard a rumor that a plan to substitute the more efficient bitumen-lamps for these cressets had been blocked by a magnate who sold firewood to Zanid.

Now and then, Fallon and his "men" halted as sounds from within the houses attracted their attention. But tonight, nothing illegal seemed to be in progress. One uproar was plainly that of a woman quarreling with her jagain; another racket was caused by a drunken party.

At its east end, Ya'fal Street bent sharply before opening out into the Square of Qarar. As Fallon neared this bend, he became aware of a noise from the square. The squad increased its gait and burst around the corner to find a crowd of Krishnans about the Fountain of Qarar and others hurrying up.

The Square of Qarar (or Garar to use the Balhibo form of the name) was not square at all, but an elongated irregular polygon. In one end lay the Fountain of Qarar, from the midst of which the statue of the Heracleian hero towered up in the moonlight over the heads of the crowd. The sculptor had portrayed Qarar as trampling on a monster, strangling another with one hand, and clutching one of his numerous lady-loves with his other arm. At the other end of the square rose the tomb of King Balade, surmounted by a statue of the great king himself seated in a pensive attitude.

Steel rang from the crowd's interior, and the moons glinted briefly on blades appearing over the heads of the mass. From the crowd, Fallon caught an occasional phrase:

"Spit the dirty Yeshtite!" " 'Ware his riposte!" "Keep your guard up!"

"Come on," said Fallon, and the four guardsmen strode forward, bills ready.

"The watch!" yelled a voice.

With amazing celerity, the crowd disintegrated, the duelling-fans running off in all directions to disappear into side-streets and alleys.

"Catch me some witnesses!" cried Fallon, and ran toward the focus of the disturbance.

As the crowd opened out, he saw that two Krishnans were fighting with swords beside the fountain—the heavy, straight cut-and-thrust rapiers of the Varasto nations.

Out of the corner of his eyes Fallon saw Qone, one of his Krishnans, catch one runaway around the ankle with the hook of his bill and pounce upon his sprawling victim. Fallon himself bored in with the intention of beating down the fighters' weapons.

Before he arrived, however, one of the two—distracted by the interruption—glanced around and away from his antagonist.

The latter instantly struck the first man's sword a terrific beat and sent it spinning away across the cobbles. Then he bounded forward and brought his blade down upon the head of his antagonist.

There goes one skull, thought Fallon. The Krishnan who had been struck fell backwards on the cobbles. His assailant stepped forward to run him through; the fatal thrust had started on its way when Fallon knocked the blade up.

With a wordless cry of rage, the duellist turned upon Fallon. The latter was being forced back by a murderously reckless attack when Cisasa, the Osirian guardsman, caught the duellist around the waist from behind with his scaly arms and tossed the fellow into the fountain. *Splash!*

Qone appeared at this point, dragging his witness by a fetter which he had snapped around the Krishnan's neck. As the dunked duellist rose like a sea-god from the waters of the fountain, Cisasa took hold of him again, hoisted him out of the water, and shook him until his belligerence subsided.

"This one iss trunk," hissed the Osirian.

The remaining Krishnan guardsman appeared at this point, panting and displaying a jacket dangling from the hook of his bill. "Mine slipped from my grasp, I grieve to say."

Fallon was bending over the corpse on the cobbles, which presently groaned and sat up, clapping hands to its bloody head. Examination showed that the folds of the fellow's stocking-turban had cushioned the blow and reduced its effect.

Fallon hauled the wounded Krishnan to his feet, saying: "This one's drunk, too. What does the witness say?"

"I saw all!" cried the witness. "Why did you trip me? I'd have come willingly. Always on the side of the law am I!"

"I know," said Fallon. "It was just an optical illusion that you were running away from us. Tell your story."

"Well, sir, the one with the cut head is a Yeshtite and the other an adherent of some new cult called Krishnan Science. They fell to disputing at Razjun's Tavern, the Krishnan Scientist holding that all evil was nonexistent, and therefore the Safq and the temple of Yesht therein had no reality, nor did the worshippers of Yesht. Well, this Yeshtite took exception and challenged . . ."

"He lies!" said the Yeshtite. "I spake no word of challenge, and did but defend myself against the villainous assault of this fap rascallion . . ."

This "fap rascallion," having coughed the water out of his windpipe, interrupted to shout: "Liar yourself! Who cast a mug of falat-wine into my face? If that be no challenge . . ."

" 'Twas but a gentle proof of my reality, you son of Myande the Execrable!" The Yeshtite, dark blood trickling down his face, blinked at Fallon and turned his wrath upon the Earthman. "A Terran creature giving commands to a loyal Balhibu in his own capital! Why go not you scrowles back to those enseamed planets whence you came? Why corrupt you our ancestral faiths with depraved, subversive heresies?"

Fallon asked, "You three can take this theologian and his pal to the House of Judgment, can't you?"

"Aye," said the Krishnan guards.

"Then take them there. I shall meet you back at the armory in time for the second round."

"Why take me?" wailed the witness. "I'm but a decent law-abiding citizen. I can be summoned any time . . ."

Fallon replied: "If you can identify yourself at the House of Judgment, they may let you go home."

Fallon watched the procession file out of the Square of Qarar, the chains of the prisoners jingling. He was glad that he did not have to go along. It was a good three-hoda hike, and the omnibus-coaches would have stopped running by now.

Moreover he was glad of a chance to visit the Safq by himself. He could do so less conspicuously in his official capacity; and to be able to do so without his fellow-guards was better yet. Luck seemed with him so far.

Anthony Fallon shouldered his bill and set off eastward. When he had gone a few blocks, the apex of the Safq began to appear over the low roofs of the intervening houses. The structure, he knew, stood just inside the boundary separating the Juru from the Bacha district, in which lay nearly all the other temples of Zanid. Religion was the business of the Bacha, just as manufacturing was that of the Izandu.

The Balhibo word *safq* means any of a family of small Krishnan invertebrates, some aquatic and some terrestrial. An ordinary land-safq looks something like a Terran snail, spiral shell and all, but instead of slithering along on a carpet of its own slime it creeps upon a myriad of small legs.

The Safq proper was an immense conical ziggurat of hand-fitted jadeite blocks, over a hundred and fifty meters high, with a spiral fluting in obvious imitation of the shell of a living safq. Its origin was lost in the endless corridors of Krishnan history. During the city-state period, following the overthrow of the Kalwm Empire by the then-barbarous Varastuma, the city of Zanid had grown up around the Safq, huddling against it until it could hardly be seen except at a distance. King Kir's great predecessor, King Balade, had cleared the buildings away from the monumental edifice and put a small park around it.

Fallon entered this park and walked slowly around the huge circumference of the Safq, ears peeled and eyes probing the structure, as if by sheer will-power he could force his vision to penetrate the stone.

It would take more than eyesight to do that, however. Various marauders had tried to bore into the structure during the last few millennia, but had been baffled by the hardness of the jadeite. As far back as historical records went, the priests of Yesht had held the Safq.

Nor was the Safq the only building owned by the cult of Yesht; there were smaller temples in Lussar, Malmaj, and other minor Balhibo cities. And beyond the little park to the east, across the boundary of the Bacha, Fallon could discern the onion-dome of the Chapel of Yesht. This was used for the minor services, to which the general public was admitted. Here were held classes for the instruction of prospective converts and other such activities. But the priests of Yesht allowed laymen into their major stronghold only on significant occasions, and then only tried and established members of the sect.

Fallon came around to the entrance, corresponding to the opening of the shell of a living safq. The beams of Karrim showed the immense bronze doors which, it was rumored, turned upon ball bearings of jewels. They still showed the marks of the futile attack by the soldiers of Ruz, hundreds of Krishnan years before. To the left of these doors something white caught Fallon's eye.

He strode closer. No sound came from inside, until he put his ear against the chilly bronze of the portal. Then something did come to him: a faint thump or bang, rhythmically repeated, but too muted by distance and thicknesses of masonry for Fallon to tell whether it was the sound of a drum, a gong, or a beaten anvil. After a while it stopped, then began again.

Fallon turned his attention from this puzzle—whose solution would no doubt transpire once he got inside the Safq—to the white thing, which comprised a number of sheets of native Krishnan paper tacked to the temple's bulletin-board with thorns of the qulaf-bush. Across the top of the board appeared the words DAKHT VA-YESHT ZANIDO. (Cathedral of Yesht in Zanid.) Fallon, though not very skilled in written Balhibou, managed to puzzle it out. The word "Yesht" was easy to pick out, for in the Balhibo print or book-hand characters it looked something like "OU62," though it read from right to left.

He strained his eyes at the sheets. The biggest said PROGRAM OF SERVICES; but despite the brightness of the double moonlight, he could not read the printing below it. (When he had been younger, he thought, he could have read it.) At last he took out his Krishnan cigar-lighter and snapped it into flame.

Then Fallon leaned against the board, got out a small pad and pencil, and copied off the wording.

Chapter IV

When Anthony Fallon walked into the armory, Captain Kordaq was sitting at the record-table—his crested helmet standing on the floor beside him and a pair of black-rimmed spectacles upon his nose—writing by lamplight. He was bringing the company rolls up to date, and looked up over the tops of his eyeglasses at Fallon. "Hail, Master Antane! Where's your squad?"

Fallon told him.

"Good—most excellent, sir. A deed of dazzling dought, worthy of a very Qarar. Take your ease." The captain picked up a jug and poured an extra cup of shurab. "Master Antane, be you not the jagain of Gazi er-Doukh?"

"Yes. How did you know?"

"Something you said."

"Why—do you know her, too?"

Kordaq sighed. "Aye. In former times I aspired to that position myself. I burned with passion like a lake of lava, but ere aught could come of it her only brother was slain and I lost touch with her. Might I impose upon your hospitality to the extent of renewing an old acquaintance some day?"

"Surely, any time. Glad to have you around."

Fallon looked toward the door as his squad trailed in to report the prisoners, and witness duly delivered to the House of

Justice. He said: "Rest your bones a minute, boys, before we start out again."

The squad sat around and drank shurab for a quarter-hour. Then another squad came in from its round, and Kordaq gave Fallon's crew its orders for the next round: "Go out via Barfur Street, then head south along the boundary of the Dumu, for Chillan's gang of rogues infests the eastern march of the Dumu . . ."

The Dumu, southernmost district of Zanid, was notorious as the city's principal thieves' quarter. Those from other sections were loud in the accusation that the criminals must have corrupted that district's watch to operate so freely. The Guard denied the charge, pleading that they were sadly undermanned.

Fallon's squad had turned off Barfur Street, and was heading along a stinking alley that zigzagged toward the district boundary, when a noise ahead made Fallon freeze in his tracks, then motion his squad forward with caution. Peering around a corner he saw a citizen backed against a wall by three characters. One covered the victim with a crossbow-pistol; another menaced him with a sword, and a third relieved him of purse and rings. The hold-up had evidently just started.

This was a rare chance. Ordinarily, a squad of the Guard arrived on the spot to find only the victim—either dead on the cobbles, or alive and yammering about the city's lawlessness.

Knowing that if he rushed directly at the criminals, they would duck into houses and alleys before he could reach them, Fallon whispered to Cisasa: "Circle around this little block on our right and take them from the other side. Just come on at full speed. When we see you, we'll jump them from here."

Cisasa faded away like a shadow. Fallon heard the slight click of the Osirian's claws on the cobbles as the dinosaurian guard went like the wind. Cisasa, Fallon knew, could outrun two normal Earthmen or Krishnans; otherwise he would not have sent him. The hold-up would have been over by the time a man could have circumambulated the block.

The click-click of claws came again, louder, and Cisasa burst into view around a bend, heading for the miscreants with Jabberwockian strides. "Come on," said Fallon.

At the scud of feet, the robbers whirled. Fallon heard the snap of the pistol's bowstring, but in the dimness he could not tell who had been shot at. There was no indication that the bolt had struck anybody.

The robbers leaped for cover. Cisasa gave an enormous bound and came down with his birdlike feet on the back of the crossbowman, hurling him prone to the ground.

The tall, thin robber with the sword, in a moment of confusion, ran toward Fallon, then skidded to a halt. Fallon thrust at the fellow with his bill, heard the clank of steel, and felt the jar down the shaft as the robber parried. Fallon's two Krishnans ran past him after the fellow who had been frisking the victim, and who had bolted past Cisasa toward an alley.

Fallon thrust and parried with his bill, pressing forward, but watching warily, lest his antagonist catch his bill-shaft with his free hand and then close in. By a fluke, he got a jab home on the fellow's sword-arm. The sword clattered to the pavement and the man turned to run. Seeing that he would have little chance of catching this lanky scoundrel in a chase, Fallon hurled his bill javelinwise. The point of the weapon struck the fellow between the shoulders. The robber ran on a couple of steps with the bill sticking in his back, then faltered and fell.

Fallon ran after him, drawing his own sword; but by the time he came up with the robber the latter was lying prone, coughing blood. The two Krishnans of the squad now reappeared from the alley into which they had chased the third thief, cursing the fellow for having given them the slip. They had recovered the citizen's purse, which the robber had dropped, but not his rings, for which he loudly berated them for inefficiency.

Roqir was rising redly over the roof-tops of Zanid when Anthony Fallon and his squad returned to the armory from their final round. They stacked their bills back in the rack and lined up to receive the nominal pay that the municipal prefect paid to members of the Guard for watch-duty.

"The stint's adjourned. Forget not Fiveday's drill," said Kordaq, handing out quarter-kard silver pieces.

"Something tells me," murmured Fallon, "that a mysterious malady will lay our gallant company low the day before the drill."

"Qarar's blood! It had better not! I shall hold you squad-leaders responsible for turning out your men."

"I'm not feeling too well myself, sir," said Fallon with a grin as he pocketed the half-kard due his rank.

"Saucy buffoon!" snorted Kordaq. "Why we tolerate your insolence I know not . . . But you'll not forget that whereof I spoke earlier, friend Antane?"

"No, no. I'll make arrangements." Fallon walked off, waving a casual farewell to the other members of his squad.

Fallon was, he supposed, foolish to spend one night out of every ten tramping the streets for a half-kard—pick-and-shovel wages. He was too self-willed and erratic to fit into a military machine, having considerable talent for command but little for obedience. And as a foreigner, he could hardly hope to rise to the top of the Balhibo tree.

Yet here he was, wearing the brassard of the Civic Guard. Why? Because a uniform had an invincible if childish fascination for him. Trailing his bill around the dusty streets of Zanid gave him, if only fleetingly, the illusion of being a potential Alexander or Napoleon. And in his present state, his ego could use all of such support that it could get.

Gazi was asleep when he plodded home, his tired brain picking at the knots of the Safq problem. She awoke as he slid into bed. "Wake me up at the end of the second hour," he mumbled, and fell asleep.

Almost at once, it seemed to him, Gazi was shaking his shoulder and telling him to get up. He had had only about three Earthly hours' sleep; but he still had to arise now to work in all the things that he meant to do this day. Knowing that he had to appear in court that afternoon, he shaved and put on his second-best suit, gulped a hasty meal, slouched out into the bright mid-morning sun, and set out for Tashin's Inn.

The A'vaz District ranged from plain slums, where it adjoined the Juru near the Balade Gate, to slums sprinkled with studios as it abutted upon the artistic and theatrical Sahi to the north. Tashin's, near the city wall on the west side of the A'vaz, was a rambling structure built (like most Balhibo houses) around a central court.

This court was filled, this morning, with the histrionic characters who made up the inn's regular clientele. A rope-walker had rigged up a rope stretching from one bit of architectural foofaraw diagonally across the court to another, and was slinking across, waving a parasol to keep his balance. A trio of tumblers were tossing one another about. On the other side of the inclosure a man rehearsed a tame gerka in its tricks. A singer practiced scales; an actor recited, with gestures.

Fallon asked the gatekeeper: "Where's Turanj the Seer?"

"Second storey, room thirteen. Go you right up."

As he started across the courtyard, Fallon was forcibly bumped by one of a trio of Krishnans. As he recovered his balance, glaring, the burly character bowed, saying: "A thousand pardons, good my sir! Tashin's wine has unsteadied my legs. Hold, are you not he with whom I got drunk at yesterday's festival?"

Simultaneously the other two closed in on the sides. The man who had bumped him was saying something genial about stepping over to Saferir's for a snort, and one of the two who had flanked him had laid a friendly hand on his left shoulder. Fallon felt, rather than saw, the razor-sharp little knife with which the third member of the trio was about to slit his purse.

Without altering his own forced smile, Fallon shouldered the Krishnans aside, took a step and then a leap, turning as he did so and whipping out his rapier, so that he came down facing all three in the guard position. He was not a little pleased with himself for still being so agile.

"Sorry, gentlemen," he said, "but I have another engagement. And I need my money, really I do."

He glanced swiftly around the courtyard. At Fallon's words there came a ripple of derisive laughter. The three thieves exchanged glowering glances and stalked out the gate. Fallon sheathed his weapon and continued on his way. For the moment, he had the crowd with him—but if he had tried to kill or arrest the thieves, or had yelled for the law, his life would not have been worth a brass arzu.

Fallon found the thirteenth room on the second level. Inside, he confronted Qais of Babaal, who had been inhaling the smoke of smoldering ramandu from a little brazier.

"Well?" asked Qais sleepily.

"I've been thinking of that offer you made me yesterday."

"Which offer?"

"The one having to do with the Safq."

"Oh. Tell me not that further reflection has braced your wavering courage."

"Possibly. I *do* mean to get back to Zamba some day, you know. But for a miserable thousand karda . . ."

"What price had you in mind?"

"Five thousand would tempt me strongly."

"*Au!* As well ask for the Kamuran's treasury entire. Though perhaps I could raise the offer by a hundred karda or so . . ."

They haggled and haggled; at last, Fallon got half of what he had at first asked, including an advance of a hundred karda to be paid at once. The twenty-five hundred karda would not, he knew, suffice in itself to put him back upon his throne. But it would do for a start. Then he said: "That's fine, Master Q—Turanj, except for one thing."

"What's that, sir?"

"For an offer of that size, I don't think it would be clever for anybody to take anybody's word—if you follow me."

Qais raised both his eyebrows and his antennae. "Sirrah! Do you imply that I, the faithful minion of great Ghuur of Qaath, would swindle you out of your price? By the nose of Tyazan, such insolence is not to be borne! I am who I am . . ."

"Now, now, calm down. After all, I might attempt a bit of swindling too, you know."

"That, Terran creature, I can well believe, were I so temerarious as to pay you in advance."

"What I had in mind was to deposit the money with some trustworthy third party."

"A stakeholder, eh? Hm. An idea, sir—but one with two patent flaws, to wit: What makes you think I bear such tempting sums about with me? And whom in this sink-hole could we trust on a matter of business concerning us of Qaath, for whom the love of the Balhibuma is something less than ardent?"

Fallon grinned. "That's something I figured out only recently. You have a banker in Zanid."

"Ridiculous!"

"Not at all, unless you've got a hoard buried in a hole in the ground. Twice, now, you've run out of money in dealing with me. Each time, you raised plenty more in a matter of an hour or two. That wouldn't have given you time to ride back to Qaath, but it would let you go to somebody in Zanid. And I know who that somebody is."

"Indeed, Master Antane?"

"Indeed. Now who in Zanid would be likely to serve you as a banker? Some financier who had cause to dislike King Kir. So I remembered what I know of Zanid's banking houses, and recalled that a couple of years ago Kastambang er-'Amirut got into trouble with the Dour. Kir had got some idea that he wanted all his visitors to approach him barefoot. Kastambang wouldn't, because he has fallen arches and it hurts him to walk without his corrective shoes. He'd loaned Kir a couple of hundred thousand karda some years before, and Kir seized upon this excuse to fine Kastambang the whole amount—and the interest, too. Kastambang has never dealt with the Dour since then, nor appeared at court. Logically he'd be your man. If he's not your banker already, he could be. In either instance, we could employ him as stakeholder."

Fallon leaned back, hands clasped behind his head, and grinned triumphantly. Qais brooded, chin in hand, then finally said: "I concede nothing, yet, save that you're a shrewd scrutator, Master Antane. You'd filch the treasure of Dakhaq from under his very nose. Before we walk out further upon the perilous Bridge of Zung that connects heaven and earth, tell me how you propose to invade the Safq."

"I thought that if we made our arrangement with Kastambang, he might know somebody who, in turn, knew the inner workings of the place. For instance if he knew of a renegade priest of Yesht—they exist, though they find it safer not to admit the fact—he or I might persuade the man to tell us . . ."

Qais interrupted: "To tell you what's in the monument? *Cha!* Why, sirrah, should I pay you in such a case? You'd run no risk.

Why should I not pay the renegade myself?"

"If you'll let me finish," said Fallon coldly. "I have every intention of examining the thing myself from the inside—no second-hand hearsay report.

"But I shall, you'll admit, have a better chance of getting out alive if I know something of the plan of the place in advance. Moreover I thought the fellow might tell us the Ritual of Yesht, so that I could slip into the temple in costume and go through a service . . . Well, further details will suggest themselves, but that gives you an idea of how I propose to start."

"Aye." Qais yawned prodigiously, forcing the sleepy Fallon to do likewise, and thrust the ramandu brazier aside. "Alack! I was just working up a most beautiful vision when your importune arrival shattered it. But duty before pleasure, my master. Let us forth."

"To Kastambang's?"

"Whither else?"

Chapter V

Out in the street, Qais hailed a khizun—an aya-drawn Balhibo hackney-carriage—and got in. Fallon's spirits rose. It had been some time since he had been able to afford a ride, and Kastambang's office lay in the commercial Kharju District, over on the far side of the city.

First they wound through the odorous alleys of the A'vaz; then through the section of the northern part of the Izandu. They emerged from this region to pass between the glitter of the theaters of the Sahi on their left and the somber bustle of the industrial Izandu on their right. Smoke arose from busy forges, and the racket of hammers, drills, files, saws, and other tools mingled in a pervasive susurration. Then they clop-clopped along a series of broad avenues which carried them through a little park, across which the wind from the steppes sent little whirls of dust dancing.

At last they plunged into the teeming magnificence of the Kharju with its shops and houses of commerce. As they angled toward the southeast, the city's one hill, crowned by the ancient castle of the kings of Balhib, rose ahead of them.

"Kastambang's," said Qais, pointing with his stick.

Fallon cheerfully let Qais pay the driver—after all, the master spy was merely dipping into the bottomless purse of Ghuur of Uriiq—and followed Qais into the building. There were the usual gatekeeper and the usual central court, variegated with tinkling fountains and statues from far Katai-Jhogorai.

Kastambang, whom Fallon had never met, proved to be an enormous Krishnan with green hair faded to pale jade, his big jowly face furrowed by sharp lines. His tun of a body was swathed in a vermilion toga in the style of Suruskand. Qais, after ceremonious introductions, said: "Sir, we would speak privily."

"Oh," said Kastambang. "We can manage, we can manage."

Without any change of expression he struck a small gong on the desk. A tailed man from the Koloft Swamps of Mikardand stuck his hairy head into the conference room.

"Prepare the lair," said the banker, then to Fallon: "Will you have a cigar, Earthman? The place will soon be ready."

The cigar proved excellent. The banker said: "Have you enjoyed our city fair on this visit, Master Turanj?"

"Aye, sir. I went to a play last night: the third of my life."

"Which one?"

"Saqqiz's *Woeful Tragedy of Queen Dejanai of Qirib*, in fourteen acts."

"Found you it effective?"

"Up till about the tenth act. After that the playwright seemed to repeat himself. Moreover, his stage was so littered with corpses that the actors playing quick characters had much ado to avoid stumbling over 'em." Qais yawned.

Kastambang made a contemptuous gesture. "Sir, this Saqqiz of Ruz is but one of these ultra-clever moderns who, having nought to say, conceal the fact by saying it in the most eccentric manner possible. You'd do better to stick to revivals of the classics, such as Harian's *Conspirators*, which opens tomorrow night."

At that moment, the Koloftu reappeared, saying: " 'Tis ready, master."

"Come, sirs," said Kastambang, heaving himself to his feet.

He proved less impressive standing than sitting, being short in the legs and moving with difficulty, wheezing and limping. He led them down the hall to a curtained doorway, the Koloftu trailing behind. A flunkey opened the door and Kastambang stood to one side, motioning them in with an expectant air. They stepped into a cage suspended in a shaft. The cage presently sank with jerks while from above came the rattle of gear-wheels. Kastambang looked at his passengers with expectation, then with a shade of disappointment. He said: "I forgot, Master Antane. Being from Earth, you must be accustomed to elevators."

"Why, yes I am," said Fallon. "But this is a splendid innovation. Reminds me of the lifts in small French hotels on Earth, with a sign saying they may be used only for going up."

The elevator stopped with a bump against a big leather cushion at the bottom of the shaft. Kastambang's elevator was, after the Safq, the leading wonder of Zanid, though Qais had ridden in it before and Fallon was hardly awed. It was raised by a couple of stalwart Koloftuma heaving on cranks, while its descent was checked by a crude brake. Fallon thought privately that it was only a matter of time before the lift-crew got careless and dropped their master to the bottom of his hidey-hole with a bang. In the meantime, however, the contraption at least saved the financier's inadequate arches.

Kastambang led his brace of guests along a dimly lighted hall, and around several corners, to a big solid qong-wood door before which stood a Balhibo arbalestier with his crossbow cocked. Fallon observed a transverse slot in the floor a few meters before he reached the door. Glancing up, he saw a matching slot in the ceiling, a portcullis, evidently. The crossbowman opened the door, which was equipped with loopholes closed on the farther side by sliding metal plates, and led the party into a small room with several more doors. A hairy Koloftu stood in front of one door with a spiked club.

This door gave into another small room, containing a man in the Moorish-looking armor of a Mikardando knight with a drawn sword. And this door let into the lair itself: an underground vault of huge cyclopean blocks, with no apertures other than the door and a couple of small ventilation holes in the ceiling.

On the stone floor stood a big table of qong-wood inlaid with other woods and with polished safq-shell in the intricate arabesque patterns of suria. Around it were ranged a dozen chairs of the same material. Fallon was glad that he had settled among the Balhibuma, who sat on chairs, rather than among some of the Krishnan nations who knelt or squatted or sat cross-legged on the floor like yogis. His joints were getting a little stiff for such gymnastics.

They sat. The Koloft man stood in the doorway.

"First," said Qais, "I should like to draw two thousand five hundred karda, gold, from my account."

Kastambang raised his antennae. "Have rumors then come to your ear that the House of Kastambang's in sore financial straits? If they have, I can assure you they're false."

"Not at all, sir. I have a special enterprise."

"Very well, good my sir," said Kastambang, scribbling a note. "Very well."

Kastambang gave directions to the Koloftu, who bowed and disappeared. Qais said: "Master Antane is undertaking a—let us say a journalistic assignment for me. He is to report to me on the interior of the Safq . . ."

Qais gave a few further details, explaining that the money was to be paid to Fallon on the completion of his task. The Koloftu came back with a bag which he set down with a ponderous clank (it weighed over seven kilos). Kastambang untied the drawstring and let the pieces spill out upon the table.

Fallon consciously kept his breath from coming faster; kept himself from leaning forward and glaring covetously at the hoard. A man could spend his whole life on Earth without seeing a golden coin; but here on Krishna, money was still hard, bright clinking stuff that weighed your pants down—real money in the ancient sense—not bits of engraved paper backed by nothing in particular. The Republic of Mikardand had once, hearing of Terran customs, tried paper money. However, the issue of notes had gotten out of hand, and the resulting runaway inflation had prejudiced all the other nations of the Triple Seas against paper money.

Fallon casually took one of the ten-kard pieces and examined it by the yellow lamp-light, turning it over as if it were of mild interest as an exotic curiosum, rather than something for which he would lie, steal, and murder—for the throne that he hoped to recover by means of it.

"Be that arrangement comfortable to you, Master Antane?" asked Kastambang. "Suits it?"

Fallon started: he had gone into a kind of trance staring at the gold piece. He pulled himself together, saying: "Certainly. First, please pay me my hundred . . . Thank you. Now let's have a written memorandum of the transaction. Nothing compromising, just a draft from Master Turanj."

"*Ohe!*" said Qais. "How shall my friend here be prevented from cashing this draft ere he's fulfilled his obligation?"

Kastambang said: "In Balhib, we observe the custom of tearing such instrument in half and giving each half to one of the parties. Thus neither can exercise his monetary power without the other. In this case, methinks we'd best tear it in three, eh?"

Kastambang opened a drawer in the table, brought out a stack of forms, and started to fill out one of them. Fallon suggested: "Leave the name of the payee blank, will you? I'll fill it in later."

"Wherefore?" asked the banker. " 'Twill not be safe, for then any knave could cash it."

"I might wish to use another name—and if it's in three pieces, it's reasonably safe. By the way, you have an account with Ta'lun and Fosq in Majbur, don't you?"

"Aye, sir, aye; we have."

"Then please make the sum payable there as well as here."

"Why, sir, why?"

"I might be leaving on a trip after this job's done," said Fallon. "And I shouldn't want to carry all that gold with me."

"Aye, folk who deal with Master Turanj do oft become appreciative of the benefits of travel." Kastambang entered a notation on the face of the instrument. When Qais had signed the paper, Kastambang folded it along two creases and tore it carefully into three pieces. One he gave to each of his visitors and one he placed in the drawer, which he locked.

Fallon asked, "In case of argument, will you arbitrate, Kastambang?"

"If Master Turanj agrees," said the Banker. Qais waved an affirmative.

"Then," said Kastambang, "you'd best meet again here in my chambers this transaction to consummate, so that I can judge how well Master Antane has carried his end of the ladder. If I award him the fillet, he can, as he likes, take the gold, or all three parts of the draft and get his money in bustling Majbur."

"Good enough," said Fallon. "And now perhaps you can help me a bit with this project."

"Eh? How?" said Kastambang suspiciously. "I am who I am: a banker, sir, a banker—no skulking intriguant . . ."

Fallon held up a hand. "No, no. I merely wondered if you, with your extensive connections, knew anybody familiar with the rituals of Yesht."

"Oho! So that's how the river runs? Aye, my connections are indeed extensive. Aye, sir, truly extensive. Now let me contemplate . . ." Kastambang put his finger-tips together, exactly as his Terran cognate might have done. "Aye, sir, I know one. Just one. But he'll not give you the secrets of the Safq proper, for he's never been within the haunted structure."

"How then does he know the ritual?"

Kastambang chuckled. "Simple. He was a priest of Yesht in Lussar, but under the influence of Terran materialism broke away, changed his identity to avoid being murdered in reprisal, and came to Zanid where he rose in the world of manufacture. As none knows his past save I, for a consideration I can—ah—persuade him to divulge the desired facts . . ."

Fallon said: "Your consideration will have to come out of the funds of Master Turanj, not out of mine."

Qais yelped a protest, but Fallon stood firm, counting on the Qaathian's avidity for the information to overcome his thrift. This course proved the correct one, for the master spy and the banker soon agreed upon the price for this transaction. Fallon asked, "Now, who's this renegade priest?"

"By Bakin, do you think me so simple as to tell you, thus giving you a hold upon him? Nay, Master Antane, nay; he's already marked as my game, not yours. Furthermore he himself would never consent so openly his past to reveal."

"What then?"

"What I'll do is this: Tomorrow evening I give an entertainment at my city house, whither this anonymous turncoat's bidden, along with many of the leading trees of Zanid." Kastambang tossed an invitation card across the table.

"Thanks indeed," said Fallon as he put the card away with studied nonchalance, hardly glancing at it. Kastambang explained: "Come, sir, and I'll thrust you and him, masked, into a room alone, so that neither shall know the other's face or have witnesses to the other's perfidy. Do you own a decent suit of festive raiment?"

"I can get by," said Fallon, mentally reviewing his wardrobe. This would be a chance to entertain Gazi in style, and stop her yammer about never going out!

"Good!" said the banker. "At the beginning of the twelfth hour on the morrow, then. Forget it not, the twelfth hour."

Krishnan law might lack the careful refinements that Earth had developed to protect the accused, but none could deny its dispatch. The duellists pleaded guilty to disorderly conduct and paid fines, in lieu of being bound over on more serious charges.

On his way out, the Yeshtite, a fellow named Girej, stopped at the witness bench and said to Fallon: "Master Antane, abject apologies for my unmannerly words last night. When I came to my senses I recalled that 'twas you who with your bill struck up the brand of the accursed Krishnan Scientist when he'd have transfixed me therewith. So thank you for my poor life."

Fallon made a never-mind gesture. "That's all right, old man; merely doing my duty."

Girej coughed. "To aby my discourtesy, perhaps you'd let me buy you a cup of kvad in slender token of my gratitude?"

"You don't even have to be grateful to do that, if you'll wait around until this next case is disposed of."

The Yeshtite agreed, and Fallon was called up to the stand to testify about the robber. (The one whom he had speared was too badly hurt to be tried, and the other was still at large.) The prisoner, one Shave, being taken *in flagrante delicto*, was tried at once and convicted.

The magistrate said: "Take him away, torture him until he reveals the name of his other accomplice, and strike off his head. Next case."

Fallon slouched out arm in arm with Girej the Yeshtite;

he always encouraged such contacts, in the hope of picking up useful information. They wandered over to a tavern where they restored their tissues while Girej garrulously reiterated his gratitude. He said: "You not only save a citizen of our fair albeit windy city, Master Antane, from an untimely and unjust end—you also saved a fellow-guardsman."

"Why, are you in the Guard too?"

"Aye, sir, and in the Juru Company, even as you are."

Fallon looked sharply at the man. "That's odd. I don't recall seeing you at any of the drills or meetings, and I don't often forget people." The last statement was no boast. Fallon had a phenomenal memory for names and faces, and knew more Krishnans in Zanid than most locally born Zaniduma.

"I have for some time been on special duty, sir."

"What do you do?"

The Yeshtite looked crafty. "Oh, I'm sworn to secrecy and so won't tell you, craving your pardon. I'll admit this much: that I guard a door."

"A door?" said Fallon. "Have another."

"Aye, a door. But never shall you learn where 'tis, or what it opens unto."

"Interesting. But look here: If this door is as important as all that, why does the government use one of us to watch it? Craving *your* pardon, of course. I should think they'd post somebody from Kir's private guard."

"They did," said Girej with a self-satisfied chuckle. "But then early this year came these alarums regarding the barbarous Ghuur of Qaath, and all the regulars have been put upon a war footing. Kir's guard's been cut to less than half, his surplus stalwarts being dispersed, some to the frontiers, others to train new levies. Hence Minister Chabarian sought out reliable members of the watch, of my religious persuasion, to take the places of the soldiery."

"What's your religious persuasion got to do with it?"

"Why, only a Yeshtite—but hold, I've spake too much already. Drink deep, my Terran friend, and foul not that long proboscis by thrusting it into matters alien to it."

And that was all that Fallon could get out of Girej, though the fellow hugged Fallon at parting and swore he'd be at his service in any future contingency.

Chapter VI

"Gazi!" called Anthony Fallon as he re-entered his house.

"Well, how now?" came her irascible voice from the back.

"Get your shawl, my pretty, for today we shop."

"But I've already marketed for the day . . ."

"No, no vulgar vegetables. I'm buying you fancy clothes."

"Art drunk again?" asked Gazi.

"How's that for a gracious response to a generous offer? No, dear. Believe it or not, we're invited to a ball."

"What?" Gazi appeared, fists on hips. "Antane, if this be another of your japes . . ."

"Me? Japes? Here, look at this!"

He showed her the invitation; Gazi threw her arms around Fallon's neck and squeezed the breath out of him. "My hero! How came you upon this? You stole it, I'll warrant!"

"Why is everybody so suspicious of me? Kastambang gave it to me with his own pudgy hand." Fallon straightened the kinks out of his vertebrae. "It's tomorrow night, so come along."

"Why the haste?"

"Don't you remember—this is bath day? We must be clean to attend this do. You don't want the banker's jagaini to sneer at you through her lorgnette—so don't forget the soap."

"The one good thing you Earthmen have brought to Krishna," she said, bustling about. "Alack! In these rags I'm ashamed to enter a good shop to purchase better garments."

"Well, I won't buy you an extra intermediate set of clothes, so you can work your way up through the shops step by step."

"And have you really the wealth for such a reckless spense?"

"Oh, don't worry. I can get the stuff at cost."

They rattled back across town, passing the Safq. Fallon gave the monstrous edifice only a cursory glance, not wishing to reveal an excessive interest in it before Gazi. Next they clattered past the House of Justice, where the heads of the day's capital offenders were just being mounted on spikes on top of a bulletin-board. Below each head, a Krishnan was writing in chalk the vital statistics and the misdeeds of its former owner.

And then into the Kharju, where the sextuple clop of the hooves of the ayas drawing the carriages of the rich mingled with the cries of newsboys selling the *Rashm*, and pushcart peddlers hawking their wares; the rustle of cloaks and skirts; the clink of scabbards; the faint rattle of bracelets and other pieces of heavy jewelry; and over it all the murmur of rolling, rhythmic sentences in the guttural, resonant Balhibo tongue.

In the Kharju, Fallon found the establishment of Ve'qir the Exclusive and pushed boldly into the hushed interior. At that moment Ve'qir himself was selling something frilly to the jagaini of the hereditary Dasht of Qe'ba, while the Dasht sat on a stool and grumped about the cost. Ve'qir glanced at Fallon, twitched his antennae in recognition, and turned back to his customer. Ve'qir's assistant, a young female, came up expectantly, but Fallon waved her aside.

"I'll see the boss himself when he's through," he said. As the assistant fell back in well-bred acquiescence, Fallon murmured into Gazi's large pointed ear: "Stop gooing over those fabrics. You'll have the old *fastuk* raising the price."

A voice said: "Hello, Mr. Fallon. Is Mr. Fallon, yes?"

Fallon spun round. There was the white-haired archeologist, Julian Fredro. Fallon acknowledged the greeting, adding: "Just sightseeing, Fredro?"

"Yes, thank you. How is project coming?"

Fallon smiled and waved toward Gazi. "Working on it now. This is my jagaini, Gazi er-Doukh." He performed the other half of the introduction in Balhibou, then switched back to English. "We're dressing her properly for a binge tomorrow night. The mad social whirl of Zanid, you know."

"Ah, you combine the business with the pleasure. Is this a part of the project?"

"Yes. Kastambang's party. He's promised me information."

"Ah? Fine. I have invitation to this party too. I shall see you there. Mr. Fallon—ah—where is this public bath I hear about, that takes place today?"

"Want to see the quaint native customs, eh? Stay with us. We're on our way to one after we finish here."

The *ci-devant* feudal lord completed his purchase, and Ve'qir came over to Fallon rubbing his hands together. Fallon demanded the best in evening wear, and presently Gazi was pirouetting slowly while Ve'qir tried one thing after another on her unclad form. Fallon chose a spangled skirt of filmy material so expensive that even Gazi was moved to protest.

"Oh, go on!" he said. "We're only middle-aged once, you know."

She threw him a look of venom but accepted the skirt. Then the couturier fitted her with a gold-lace *ulemda* set with semi-precious stones—a kind of harness or halter worn by upper-class Balhibo women on the upper torso on formal occasions, adorning without concealing.

At last Gazi stood in front of the mirror, turning slowly this way and that. "For this," she said to Fallon, "I'd forgive you much. But since you're so rich for the nonce, why get you not something for yourself? 'Twould pleasure me to pick a garment for you."

"Oh, I don't need anything new. And it's getting late . . ."

"Yes you do, my love. That old rain-cloak of yours is unfit for the veriest beggar, so patched and darned is it."

"Oh, all right." With money in his scrip, Fallon could not long withstand the urge to buy. "Ve'qir, have you got a man's rain-cloak in stock? Nothing fancy—just good sound middle-class stuff."

Ve'qir, as it happened, had.

"Very well," said Fallon, having tried on the garment. "Add it up, and don't forget my discount."

Fallon completed his purchases, hailed a khizun, and started back toward the Juru with both Gazi and Fredro. Gazi said: " 'Tis unwontedly open-handed of you, my love. But tell me, how got you such a vast reduction from Ve'qir, who's known for squeezing the last arzu from those so mazed by the glamor of his reputation as to venture into his lair?"

Fallon smiled. "You see," he said, repeating each phrase in two languages, "Ve'qir the Exclusive had an enemy—one Hulil, who preceded Chillan as Zanid's leading public menace. This Hulil was blackmailing Ve'qir. Then the silly ass leaned too far out of a window and broke his skull on the flagstones below. Well, Ve'qir insists that I had something to do with it, though I proved to the prefect's investigators that, at the time, I was in conference with Percy Mjipa and couldn't have pushed the blighter."

As they passed the Safq, Fredro craned his neck to stare at it and began to babble naively about getting in, until Fallon kicked his shins. Fortunately Gazi knew a mere half-dozen words of English, all of them objectionable.

"Where we going?" asked Fredro.

"To my house to drop off these packages and put on our *sufkira*."

"Please, can we not stop to look at Safq?"

"No, we should miss our bath."

Fallon glanced at the sun with concern, wondering if he was not late already. He had never gotten altogether used to doing without a watch; and the Krishnans, though they now made crude wheeled clocks, had not yet attained to watch-culture.

Gazi and Fredro kept Fallon busy interpreting, for Gazi knew practically nothing of the Terran tongues and Fredro's Balhibou was still rudimentary; but Fredro was full of questions about Krishnan housewifery, while Gazi was eager to impress the visitor. She tried to disguise her embarrassment when they stopped in front of the sad-looking little brick house that Fallon called home, jammed in between two larger houses, and with big cracks running across the tiles where the building had settled unevenly. It did not even have a central court, which in Balhib practically relegated it to the rank of hovel.

"Tell him," Gazi urged, "that we do but dwell here for the

nonce, till you can find a decent place to suit us."

Fallon, ignoring the suggestion, led Fredro in. In a few minutes, he and Gazi reappeared, clad in sufkira—huge togalike pieces of towelling wrapped around their bodies.

"It's only a short walk," said Fallon. "Be good for you."

They walked east along Asada Street until this thoroughfare joined Ya'fal Street coming up from the southwest and turned into the Square of Qarar. As they walked, more people appeared, until they were engulfed in a sufkid-wrapped crowd.

Scores of Zaniduma were already gathered in the Square of Qarar where, only the night before, Fallon and his squad had stopped the sword-fight. There were but few non-Krishnans in sight; many non-Krishnan races did not care for the Balhibo bath-customs. Osirians, for example, had no use for water at all, but merely scrubbed off and replaced their body-paint at intervals. Thothians, expert swimmers, insisted on total immersion. And most human beings, unless they had become well assimilated to Krishnan ways, or came from some country like Japan, observed their planet's tabu against public exposure.

The water-wagon, drawn by a pair of shaggy, six-legged shaihans, stood near the statue of Qarar. The cobbles shone where they had been watered down and scrubbed by the driver's assistant, a tailed Koloftu of uncommon brawn, now securing his long-handled scrubbing-brush to the side of the vehicle.

The driver himself had climbed up on top of the tank and was extending the shower-heads over the crowd. Presently he called out: "Get ye ready!"

There was a general movement. Half the Krishnans took off their sufkira and handed them to the other half. The unclad ones crowded forward to get near the shower-heads, while the rest wormed their way back toward the outer sides of the square.

Fallon handed his sufkir to Fredro, saying: "Here, hold these for us, old man!"

Gazi did likewise. Fredro looked a little startled but took the garments, saying: "Used to do something like this in Poland before period of Russian domination two centuries ago. Russians claimed it was *nye kulturno*. I suppose one cannot have the bath without someone to hold these things?"

"That's right. The Zaniduma are a light-fingered lot. This'll be almost the first time Gazi and I have been able to take our bath at the same time. If you'd like to take yours afterward . . ."

"No thank you! Is running water in hotel."

Fallon, holding the family cake of soap in one hand, and towing Gazi with the other, wormed his way toward the nearest shower-head. The driver and his assistant had finished tightening the joints of their extensible pipe-system and now laid hold of the handles at the ends of the walking-beam that worked the pump. They tugged these handles up and down, grunting, and presently the shower-heads sneezed and began to spray water.

The Zaniduma yelled as the cold fluid struck their greenish skins. They laughed and splashed each other; it was a festive occasion. The land of Zanid rose out of the treeless prairies of west-central Balhib, not many hundred hoda from where these gave way to the vast dry steppes of Jo'ol and Qaath. Water for the city had to be hauled up from deep wells, or from the muddy trickle of the shallow Eshqa. There was a water-main from the Eshqa above the city and a system of shaihan-powered pumps for raising the water, but this served only the royal palace, the Terran Hotel, and a few of the mansions in the Gabanj.

Fallon and Gazi had gotten reasonably clean, and were picking their way out of the crowd, when Fallon stiffened at the sight of Fredro, on the edge of the square, with their two sufkira draped over one shoulder, focussing his camera for a shot of the crowd.

"Oy!" said Fallon. "The damned fool doesn't know about the soul-fraction belief!"

He started toward the archeologist, pulling Gazi, when she pulled back, saying: "Look! Who's that, Antane?"

A voice resounded through the square. Turning, Fallon saw, over the heads of the Krishnans, that an Earthman in a black suit and a white turban had climbed up on the wall around the base of the tomb of King Balade, to harangue the bathers:

". . . for this one God hates all forms of immodesty. Beware, sinful Balhibuma, lest ye mend not your iniquitous ways, and He deliver you into the hands of the Qaathians and the Gozashtanduma. Dirt is a thousand times better than exposure to . . ."

It was Welcome Wagner, the American Ecumenical-Monotheist. Fallon observed that the heads of the Krishnans were turning, one by one, toward the source of this stentorian outcry.

". . . for in the Book, it says that no person shall expose his or her modesty before another. And furthermore . . ."

"Is *everybody* trying to start a riot?" sighed Fallon. He turned back toward Fredro, who was aiming his camera at the backs of the crowd, and hurried over to the archeologist, barking: "Put that thing away, you idiot!"

"What?" asked Fredro. "Put away camera? Why?"

The crowd, still looking at Wagner, began to grumble. Wagner kept on in his piercing rasp:

"Nor shall ye eat the flesh of those creatures ye call safqa, for it was revealed that the One God deems sin the eating of those Terran creatures called snails, clams, oysters, scallops, and other animals of the shellfish kind . . ."

Fallon said to Fredro: "The Balhibuma believe that taking a picture of them steals a piece of their souls."

"But that cannot be the right. I took—I took pictures at festival and nobody minded."

Some of the crowd had begun to answer, "We'll eat as pleases us!" "Go back to the planet whence you came!"

Fallon said tensely: "They had their clothes on! The tabu applies only when they're stripped!"

The crowd had become noisier, but Welcome Wagner merely yelled louder. The driver of the water-wagon and his assistant, becoming absorbed in the scene, stopped pumping. When the water ceased to flow, those who had been standing around the wagon began straggling across the square to the denser crowd that was forming around the tomb.

Fredro said: "Just one more picture, please."

Fallon impatiently grabbed for the camera. Instead of letting go, Fredro tightened his grip upon the device, shouting: *"Psiakrew!* What you doing, fool?"

As they struggled for possession of the camera, the sufkira slid off Fredro's shoulder to the ground. Gazi, with an exclamation of irk (for she would have to wash the garments) picked them up. Meanwhile Fredro's shout, and the struggle between the archeologist and Fallon, had drawn the attention of the nearer Zaniduma. One of the latter pointed and cried: "Behold these other Earthmen! One of them is trying to steal our souls!"

"Oh, he is, is he?" said another.

Glancing around, Fallon saw that he and his party had in their turn become the focus of hostile glances. Around the tomb of Balade, the noise of the hecklers had nearly drowned out the powerful voice of Welcome Wagner. That crowd was working itself up to the stage where they would soon pull the Earthman down off the wall and beat him to death, if they did not kill him in some more lingering and humorous manner. Even the water-wagon driver and his assistant had gotten down off the vehicle and trailed over to see what was happening.

Fallon jerked Fredro's sleeve. "Come on, you idiot. Shift-ho!"

"Where?" asked Fredro.

"Oh, to hell with you!" cried Fallon, ready to dance with

exasperation.

He caught Gazi's wrist and started to lead her toward the water-wagon. A Zanidu stepped up close to Fredro, stuck out his tongue, and shouted: *"Bakhan Terrao!"*

The Krishnan aimed a slap at the archeologist's face. Fallon heard the slap connect, and then the more solid sound of Fredro's fist. He glanced back to see the Zanidu fall backwards to a sitting position on the cobbles. The scientist, if elderly, still had plenty of steam left in his punches.

The other Zaniduma began to close in, shouting and waving their fists. Fredro, as if aware for the first time of the trouble that he had fomented, started after Fallon and Gazi. The little camera swung on the end of its strap as Fredro turned as he ran, shouting polysyllabic Polish epithets.

"The wagon!" said Fallon to his jagaini.

Reaching the water-wagon, Gazi turned long enough to toss the bundle of towelling into Fallon's hands, and swung herself up on to the driver's seat by the hand-holds. Then she held out her hands for the sufkira, which Fallon threw to her before climbing up himself. Right after him, came the bulky body of Julian Fredro.

Fallon pulled the whip out of its socket, cracked it over the heads of the shaihans, and shouted: *"Hao! Haoga-i!"*

The bulky brutes stirred their twelve legs and lunged forward against their harness. The wagon started with a jerk. At that moment, Fallon had no particular thought of interfering in the quarrel between the citizens of Zanid and Welcome Wagner. However, the wagon happened to be headed straight for this scene of strife, so that Fallon could not help seeing that bare arms were reaching up from the crowd and trying to pull down the preacher, who clung to the top of the wall, still shouting.

Little though he really cared about Wagner's fate, Fallon could not resist the temptation to try to cut a fine figure in the sight of Gazi and Fredro. He cracked his whip once more, yelling: *"Vyant-hao!"*

At the cry, the rearmost Zaniduma turned and tumbled out of the way as the team lumbered in among them.

"Vyant-hao!" screamed Fallon, cracking his whip over the heads of the throng.

Chapter VII

The wagon drove in among the crowd, dividing it as a ship does flotsam, while the Balhibuma who had started to chase Fredro ran in behind it, shouting threats and objurgations. Under Fallon's guidance the wagon slewed up against the wall around the tomb, like a motorboat coming in to dock, where Welcome Wagner was shakily getting to his feet again.

"Jump aboard!" yelled Fallon.

Wagner jumped, almost falling off on the far side of the water-tank. A few more cracks of the whip, and the team broke into a shambling run for the nearest exit from the Square of Qarar.

"Au!" shrieked the driver. "Come back with my wagon!"

The driver ran up alongside the wagon and began to swing himself aboard. Fallon hit him a sharp rap over the head with the butt of the whip, at which he fell back upon the cobbles. A glance to the rear showed Fallon that several others were trying to climb up also, but Fredro got rid of one by kicking him in the face while Wagner stamped on the fingers of another as he grasped one of the hand-holds. Fallon leaned forward and snapped his whip against the bare hide of yet another, who was trying to seize the bridle of one of the animals. With a howl, the Krishnan hopped away to nurse his welt.

Fallon urged the shaihans to greater speed as the wagon rumbled into the nearest street. It seemed to Fallon that half the people of Zanid must be chasing his vehicle. But with the water-tank three-quarters empty, the team made good speed, sending chance pedestrians leaping for safety.

"Where—where are we going?" asked Gazi.

"Away from that mob," growled Fallon, jerking his thumb back toward the horde. "Hold on!"

He pulled the team into a tight turn around a corner, so that the wagon rocked and skidded perilously. Then he did another, and another, zigzagging until, despite his own familiarity with the city, he was a bit confused himself as to where he was. A few more turns and the mob seemed to have been left behind, so he let the team drop back to their six-legged trot.

People along the street stared with interest as the water-wagon went by, bearing three Earthmen—two in their native costume and one nude, and an equally unclad Krishnan woman.

Wagner spoke up: "Well, say, I don't know who you are, but I'm glad you got me out of that. I guess I hadn't ought to have stirred up these heathens so. They're kind of excitable."

Fallon said: "My name's Fallon, and these are Gazi er-Doukh and Dr. Fredro."

"Pleased to meet you," said Wagner. "Say, aren't you two gonna put your clothes back on?"

"When we get around to it," said Fallon.

"It makes us kind of conspicuous," said Wagner.

Fallon was about to reply that nothing prevented Wagner from getting off, when the wagon rumbled into the park around the Safq. Fredro gave an exclamation.

Wagner looked at the looming structure, and he shook a fist, crying: "If I could blow up that lair of heathen idolatry, I wouldn't care none if I got blown up with it!"

"What?" cried Fredro. "You crazy? Blow up priceless archeological treasure?"

"I don't care nothing about your atheistic science."

"Ignorant savage," said Fredro.

"Ignorant, huh?" said Wagner with heat. "Well, your so-called science don't mean a blessed thing, mister. You see, *I* know the *truth*, so that puts me ahead of you no matter how many of them college degrees you got."

"Shut up, you two," said Fallon. *"You're* making us conspicuous."

"I will not shut up," said Wagner. "I bear witness to the truth, and I won't be silenced by the ignorant tongues of . . ."

"Then get off the wagon," interrupted Fallon.

"I will not! It ain't your wagon neither, mister, and I got as much right on it as you."

Fallon caught Fredro's eye. *"Abwerfen ihn, ja?"*

"Jawohl!" said the Pole.

"Catch," said Fallon to Gazi, tossing her the reins.

Then he and Fredro each caught one of Welcome Wagner's arms. The muscular evangelist braced himself to resist, but the double attack was too much for him. A grunt and a heave, and Wagner flew off the top of the water-tank to land on his white turban in a spacious puddle of muddy water.

Splash!

Fallon took back the reins and speeded up the shaihans lest Wagner run after to try to clamber back aboard. He took one last look back around the water-tank. Wagner was sitting in the puddle, head bowed, and beating the brown water with his fists. He seemed to be crying.

Fredro smiled. "Good for him! Crazy fools like that, who want to blow up a monument, should be boiled in oil." He clenched his fists. "When I think of such crazy fools, I—I . . ." He ground his teeth audibly as his limited English failed him.

Fallon pulled up to the curb, stopped the shaihans, and set the brake. "Best leave this here."

"Why not ride it to your house?" asked Fredro.

"Haven't you ever heard that American expression, 'Don't steal chickens close to home'?"

"No. What does it mean, please?"

Fallon, wondering how so educated a man could be such a

fool, explained why he would not park the vehicle right in front of his own domicile, to be found by the prefect's men when they scoured the Juru for it. As he explained, he climbed down from the water-wagon and donned his sufkir.

"Care to drop in on us for a spot of kvad, Fredro? I could do with one after this afternoon's events."

"Thank you, no. I must get back to my hotel to develop my photos. And I am—ah—dining with Mr. Consul Mjipa tonight."

"Well, give Percy Pickle-face my love. You might suggest he find an excuse for cancelling the Reverend Wagner's passport. That bloke damages Balhibo-Terran relations more with one sermon than Percy can make up for by a hundred good-will gestures."

"That wretched obscurantist! I will do. Is funny. I know some Ecumenical Monotheists on Earth. While I don't believe their teachings, or approve of their movement, none is like this Wagner. He is a class of himself."

"Well," said Fallon, "I suppose at this distance they don't feel they can import missionaries specially, so they grab anybody here who shows willingness and send him out after souls. And speaking of souls, *don't* try to photograph a naked Balhibu! At least not without his or her permission. That's as bad as the sort of thing Wagner does."

Fredro's face took on the look of a puppy surprised in a heinous deed. "I was stupid, yes? Will you excuse, please? I will not do it again. A burnt child is twice shy."

"Eh? Oh, surely. Or if you must photograph them, use one of those little Hayashi ring-cameras."

"They do not take a very clear picture, but . . . And thank you again. I—I am sorry to be such a trouble." Fredro glanced back along the street by which they had driven, and a look of horror came over his face. "Oh, look who is coming! *Dubranec!*"

He turned and walked off rapidly. Fallon said: *"Nasuk genda"* in Balhibou, then looked in the direction indicated. To his astonishment, he saw Welcome Wagner running toward him, his muddy turban still on his head.

"Hey, Mr. Fallon!" said Wagner. "Looky, I'm sorry we had this here little trouble. I get so riled up when something goes against my principles that I don't hardly know what I'm doing."

"Well?" said Fallon, looking at Wagner as if the latter had crawled out from under a garbage pile.

"Well, what I mean is, do you mind if I walk home with you? And pay a visit to your place for a little while? Please?"

"Everybody's apologizing to me today," said Fallon. "Why should you wish to call on me, of all people?"

"Well, you see, when I was sitting there in the street after you threw me off, I heard a crowd of people—and sure enough there came all that mob of naked Krishnans some of 'em with clubs even. They musta trailed us by asking which way the wagon went. So I thought it might be safer if I could get indoors for a while, until they give up looking. Them heathens looked like they was stirred up real mean."

"By all means, let's move," said Fallon, setting out at a brisk walk and dragging Gazi after him. "Come along, Wagner. You caused most of this trouble, but I wouldn't leave you to the mob. Krishnan mobs can do worse things even than Terran ones."

They walked as fast as they could without breaking into a run the few blocks to Fallon's house. Here Fallon shepherded the other two in and closed and locked the door behind them.

"Wagner, bear a hand with this couch. I'm moving it against the door, just in case."

The settee was placed in front of the door.

"Now," said Fallon, "you stay here and look out while we get dressed."

A few minutes later, Fallon had donned his diaper and Gazi a skirt. Fallon came back into the living room. "Any sign of our friends?"

"Nope. No sign," said Wagner.

Fallon held out a cigar. "Do you smoke? Thought not." He lit the cigar himself and poured a drink of kvad. "Same with alcohol?"

"Not for me, but you go ahead. I wouldn't try to tell you what to do in your own house, even if you are committing a sin."

"Well, that's something, Dismal Dan."

"Oh, you heard about that? Sure, I used to be the biggest sinner in the Cetic planets—maybe in the whole galaxy. You got no idea of the sins I committed." Wagner sighed wistfully, as if he would like to commit some of these sins over again for old times' sake. "But then I seen the light. Miss Gazi . . ."

"She doesn't understand you," said Fallon.

Wagner switched to his imperfect Balhibou. "Mistress Gazi, I wanted to say, you just don't know what real happiness is until you see the light. All these material mundane pleasures pass away like a cloud of smoke in the glory of Him who rules the universe. You know all these gods you got on Krishna? They don't exist, really, unless you want to say that when you worship the god of love you worship an aspect of the true God, who is also a God of Love. But if you're going to worship an aspect of the true God, why not worship all of Him . . ."

Fallon, nursing his drink, soon became bored with the homily. However, Gazi seemed to be enjoying it, so Fallon put up with the sermon to humor her. He admitted that Wagner had a good deal of magnetism when he chose to turn it on. The man's long nose quivered, and his brown eyes shone with eagerness to make a convert. When Fallon tossed in an occasional question or objection, Wagner buried him under an avalanche of dialectics, quotations, and exhortations which he could not have answered had he wished.

After more than an hour of this, however, Roqir had set and the Zanido mob had not materialized. Fallon, growing hungry, broke into the conversation to say: "I hope you don't mind my throwing you out, old man, but . . ."

"Oh, sure, you gotta eat. I forget myself when I get all wrapped up in testifying to the truth. Of course I don't mind taking pot-luck with you, if you aren't gonna serve safqa or ambara . . ."

"It's nice to have seen you," said Fallon firmly, pulling the sofa away from the door. "Here's your turban, and watch out for temptation."

With a sigh, Wagner wound the long dirty strip of white cloth around his lank black hair. "Yeah, I'll go, then. But here's my card." He handed over a pasteboard printed in English, Portuguese, and Balhibou. "That address is a boarding-house in the Dumu. Any time you feel low in the spirit, just come to me and I'll radiate you with divine light."

Fallon said: "I suggest that you'll get further with the Krishnans if you don't start by insulting their ancient customs, which are very well adapted to their kind of life."

Wagner bowed his head. "I'll try to be more tactful. After all I'm just a poor, fallible sinner like the rest of us. Well, thanks again. G'bye and may the true God bless you."

"Thank Bakh he's gone!" said Fallon. "How about some food?"

"I'm preparing it now," said Gazi. "But I think you do Master Wagner an injustice. At least he seems to be that rarity: a man unmoved by thoughts of self."

Fallon, though a little unsteady from all the kvad that he had drunk during Wagner's harangue, poured himself another. "Didn't you hear the *zaft* inviting himself to dinner? I don't trust these people who claim to be so unselfish. Wagner was an adventurer, you know—lived by his wits, and I should say he was still doing it."

"You judge everybody by yourself, Antane, be they Terran or Krishnan. I think Master Wagner is at base a good man, even though his methods be rash and injudicious. As for his theology I know not, but it might be true. At least his arguments sounded no whit more fallacious than those of the followers of Bakh, Yesht, Qondyor, and the rest."

Fallon frowned at his drink. His jagaini's admiration for the despised Wagner nettled him, and alcohol had made him rash. To impress Gazi, and to change the subject to one wherein he could shine to better advantage, he broke his rule about never discussing business with her by saying: "By the way, if my present deal goes through, we should have Zamba practically wrapped up and tied with string."

"What now?"

"Oh, I've made a deal. If I furnish some information to a certain party, I shall be paid enough to start me on my way."

"What party?"

"You'd never guess. A mere mountebank and charlatan to all appearances, but he commands all the gold of Dakhaq. I met him at Kastambang's this morning. Kastambang wrote out a draft, and he signed it, and the banker tore it into three parts and gave us each one. So if anybody can get all three parts, he can cash it either here or in Majbur."

"How exciting!" Gazi appeared from the kitchen. "May I see?"

Fallon showed her his third of the draft, then put it away. "Don't tell anybody about this."

"I'll not."

"And don't say I never confide in you. Now, how long before dinner?"

Chapter VIII

Fallon was halfway through his second cup of shurab, the following morning, when the little brass gong suspended by the door went *bonggg*. The caller was a Zanido boy with a message. When he had sent the boy off with a five-arzu tip, Fallon read:

Dear Fallon: Fredro told me last night of your plans to attend Kastambang's party tonight. Could you get around to see me today, bringing your invitation with you? Urgent.
P. Mjipa, Consul

Fallon scowled. Did Mjipa propose to interfere in his plans on some exalted pretext that Fallon would lower the prestige of the human race before "natives"? No, he could hardly do that and at the same time urge Fallon to proceed with the Safq project. And Fallon had to admit that the consul was an upright and truthful representative of the human species.

So he had better go to see what Percy Mjipa had in mind, especially as he really had nothing better to do that morning. Fallon accordingly stepped back into his house to gather his gear.

"What is't?" asked Gazi, clearing the table.

"Percy wants to see me."

"What about?"

"He doesn't say."

Without further explanation, Fallon set forth, the invitation snug in the wallet that swung from his girdle. Feeling less reckless with his money than he had the previous day, he caught an ominibus drawn by a pair of heavy draft-ayas on Asada Street over to the Kharju, where the Terran Consulate stood across the street from the government office building. Fallon waited while Mjipa held a long consultation with a Krishnan from the prefect's office.

When the prefect's man had gone, Mjipa called Fallon into his inner office and began in his sharp, rhythmic tones: "Fredro tells me you're taking Gazi to this binge at Kastambang's. Is that right?"

"Right as rain. And how does that concern the Consulate?"

"Have you brought your invitation as I asked you to?"

"Yes."

"May I see it, please?"

"Look here, Percy, you're not going to do anything silly like tearing it up, are you? Because I'm working on that blasted project of yours. No party, no Safq."

Mjipa shook his head. "Don't be absurd." He scrutinized the card. "I thought so."

"You thought what?"

"Have you read this carefully?"

"No. I speak Balhibou fluently enough, but I don't read it very well."

"Then you didn't read this line, *'Admit one only'*?"

"What?"

Mjipa indicated the line in question. Fallon read with a sinking heart. *"Fointsaq!"* he cried in tones of anguish.

Mjipa explained: "You see, I know Kastambang pretty well. He belongs to one of these disentitled noble families. A frightful snob—even looks down on *us*, if you can imagine such cheek. I'd seen one of his *'Admit one only'* cards and I didn't think he would want Gazi—a brotherless, lower-class woman. So I thought I'd warn you to save you embarrassment later if you both showed up at his town house and the flunkey wouldn't let her in."

Fallon stared blankly at Mjipa's face. He could see no sign of gloating. Hence, while he hated to admit it, it looked as though the consul had really done him a kindness.

"Thanks," said Fallon finally. "Now all I have to do is break the news to Gazi without getting my own neck broken in the process. I shall need the wisdom of 'Anerik to get me out of this one."

"I can't help you there. If you must live with these big brawny Krishnan women . . ."

Fallon refrained from remarking that Mjipa's wife was built on the lines of the elephants of her native continent. He asked: "Will you be there?"

"No. I wangled invitations for myself and Fredro, but he decided against going."

"Why? I should think he'd drool over the prospect."

"He heard about the beast-fights they stage at these things, and he hates cruelty. As for me, these brawls merely make my head ache. I'd rather stay home reading *'Abbeq and Dangi'.*"

"In the original Gozashtandou? All two hundred and sixty-four cantos?"

"Certainly," said Mjipa.

"Gad, what a frightful fate to be an intellectual! By the bye, you said something the other day about getting me some false feelers and things for disguises."

"A good thing you reminded me." Mjipa dug into a drawer and brought out a package. "You'll find enough cosmetics to disguise both of you: hair-dye, ears, antennae, and so on. As Earthmen practically never use them in Balhib any more, you should be able to get away with it."

"Thanks. Cheerio, Percy."

Fallon strolled out, thinking furiously. First he suppressed, not without a struggle, an urge to get so drunk that the accursed party would be over and done with by the time he sobered up. Then, as the day was a fine one, he decided to spend some time walking along the city wall instead of returning directly home.

He did not wish to quarrel or break up with Gazi; on the other hand there would certainly be fireworks if he simply told her the truth. He was plainly in the wrong for not having puzzled out the meaning of all the squiggles on the card. Of course he had shown it to her, so she should also have seen the fatal phrase. But it would do no good to tell her that.

The nearest section of the wall lay to the east, directly away from his home, where the wall extended from the palace on the hill to the Lummish Gate. Most of the space from the fortifications surrounding the palace grounds to the Lummish Gate was taken up by the barracks of the regular army of Balhib. These barracks were occupied by whichever regiment happened to be on capital duty, plus officers and men on detached service. These last included Captain Kordaq, assigned the command of the Juru Company of the Civic Guard.

Thinking of Kordaq set off a new train of speculation. Perhaps, if he worked it right . . .

He inquired at the barracks and presently the captain appeared, polishing his spectacles.

"Hello, Kordaq," said Fallon. "How's life in the regular army?"

"Greeting, Master Antane! To answer your question, though 'twere meant as mere courteous persiflage: 'tis onerous, yet not utterly without compensation."

"Any more rumors of wars?"

"In truth the rumors continued to fly like insensate aqebats, yet no thicker than before. One becomes immunized, as when one has survived the bambir-plague one need never fear it again. But, sir, what brings you hither to this grim edifice?"

Fallon replied: "I'm in trouble, my friend, and you're the only one who can help me out."

"Forsooth? Though grateful for the praise implied by your confidence, yet do I hope you'll not lean too heavily upon this frail swamp-reed."

Fallon candidly explained his blunder, and added: "Now, you've been wanting to renew your acquaintance with Mistress Gazi, yes?"

"Aye, sir, for old times' sake."

"Well, if I went home sick and took to bed, of course Gazi would be much disappointed."

"Meseems she would," said Kordaq. "But why all this tumultation over a mere entertainment? Why not simply tell her straight you cannot go, and carry her elsewhither?"

"Ah, but I've *got* to attend, whether she goes or not. Matter of business."

"Oh. Well then?"

"If you accidentally dropped in at my house during the eleventh hour, you could soothe the invalid and then offer to console Gazi by taking her out yourself."

"So? And whither should I waft this pretty little ramand useed?"

Fallon suppressed a smile at the thought of Gazi's heft. "There's a revival of Harian's *The Conspirators* opening in the Sahi tonight. I'll pay for the seats."

Kordaq stroked his chin. "An unusual offer, but—by Bakh, I'll do it, Master Antane! Captain Kyum owes me an evening's duty with the Guard. I'll send him to the armory in my stead. During the eleventh hour, eh?"

"That's right. And there's no hurry about bringing her home early, either." At the gleam in Kordaq's eye, Fallon added: "Not, you understand, that I'm making you a present of her!"

Fallon got home for lunch, finding Gazi still in her sunny mood. After lunch, he settled down with a copy of Zanid's quintan newspaper, the *Rashm,* a mythological name that might be roughly translated as "Stentor." Soon he began to complain of feeling ill. "Gazi, what *was* in that food?"

"Nought out of the ordinary, dear one. The best badr and a fresh-killed ambar."

"Hmp." Fallon had gotten over the squeamishness of Earthmen towards eating the ambar, an invertebrate something like a lobster-sized roach. But since the creature decayed rapidly it would make a good excuse. A little later, he began to writhe and groan, to Gazi's patent alarm. When another hour had passed he was back in bed, looking stricken, while Gazi in her disappointment dissolved into a fit of hysterical weeping, beating the wall with her fists.

When her shrieks and sobs had subsided enough to enable her to speak articulately, she wailed: "Surely the God of the Earthmen is set against our enjoying a moiety of harmless pleasure! And all that lovely gold squandered on my new clothes, now never to be worn! Would we'd placed it at interest in a sound bank."

"Oh, we'll—unh—find an occasion for them," said Fallon, grunting with simulated pain. His feeble conscience pricked him at this point. He felt that he had never given Gazi credit for her virtue of thrift; she had a much more acute sense of the value of a kard than he.

"Don't worry," he said. "I shall be well by the tenth hour."

"Shall I fetch Qouran the Physician?"

"I wouldn't let one of your Krishnan doctors lay a finger on me. They're apt to take out an Earthman's liver in the belief it's his appendix."

"There's a physician of your own kind, a Dr. Nung, in the Gabnj. I could fetch him . . ."

"No, I'm not that badly off. Besides, he's a Chinese and would probably feed me ground yeki-bones." (This was hardly fair to Dr. Nung, but served as an excuse.)

Fallon found the rest of the long afternoon very dull, for he did not dare to read, lest he give the impression of feeling too well. When the time for his third meal came he said that he did not wish any food. This alarmed Gazi—used to his regular and hearty appetite—more than his groans and grimaces.

After an interminable wait, the light of Roqir dimmed and the door-gong bonged. Gazi hastily wiped away her remaining tears and went to the door. Fallon heard voices from the vestibule, and in came Captain Kordaq.

"Hail, Master Antane!" said this last. "Hearing you were indisposed, I came to offer such condolence as my rough taciturn soldier's tongue is capable of. What ails my martial comrade?"

"Oh, something I ate. Nothing serious—I shall be up by tomorrow. Do you know my jagaini, Gazi er-Doukh?"

"Surely. We were formerly fast friends and recognized each other at the door, not without a melancholy pang for all the years that have passed since last we saw each other. 'Tis a pleasure to encounter her once again after so long a lapse." The captain paused as if in embarrassment. "I had a small unworthy offer of entertainment to proffer—seats to the opening of *The Conspirators*—but if you're too unwell . . ."

"Take Gazi," said Fallon. "We were going to Kastambang's party, but I can't make it."

There was a lot of polite cross-talk, Gazi saying that she would not leave Fallon sick, and Fallon—supported by Kordaq—insisting that she go. She soon gave in and prepared to be on her way in her spangled transparent skirt and glittering ulemda.

Fallon called: "Mind that you take your raincoat. I don't care if there isn't a cloud in the sky. I don't want to take a chance of getting those new clothes wet!"

As soon as they were out of the house, Fallon bounded out of bed and dressed in his best tunic and diaper. This was going to turn out better than he had thought. For one thing, even if he had been able to take Gazi to Kastambang's, having to look out for her would have hampered him in his project.

For another, she had been hinting that she would like to be taken to *The Conspirators*. And Fallon, having seen *The Conspirators* once in Majbur, had no wish to witness the drama again.

Fallon wolfed some food, buckled on his sword, took a quick swig of kvad and a quick look at himself in the mirror, and set out for the mansion of Kastambang the banker.

Chapter IX

Hundreds of candles cast their soft light upon the satiny evening-tunics of the male Krishnans and upon the bare shoulders and bosoms of the females. Jewels glittered; noble metals gleamed.

Watching the glitter, Fallon (not normally a very cogitative man) asked himself: These people are being pitchforked from feudalism into capitalism in a few years. Will they go on to a socialist or communist stage, as some Terran nations did, before settling down to a kind of mixed economy? The inequality of wealth might be considered an incitement to such a revolutionary tendency. But then, Fallon reflected, the Krishnans had shown themselves so far too truculent, romantic, and individualistic to take kindly to any collectivist régime.

He sat by himself, sipping the mug of kvad that he had obtained from the bar and watching the show on the little stage. If Gazi had been here, he would have had to dance with her in the ballroom, where a group of Balhibo musicians was giving a spiritedly incompetent imitation of a Terran dance-band. As Anthony Fallon danced badly and found the sport a bore, his present isolation did not displease him.

On the stage, a couple who advertised themselves as Ivan and Olga were leaping, bounding, and kicking up their booted feet in a Slavonic type of buck-and-wing. Although they wore rosy make-up over their greenish skins, had their antennae pasted down to their foreheads, and concealed their elvish ears, the male by pulling his sheepskin Cossack hat down over them and the female by her coiffure, Fallon could see from small anatomical details that they were Krishnans. Why did they pretend to be Terrans? Because, no doubt, they made a better living that way; to Krishnans, the Earth (and not their own world) was the place of glamor and romance.

A hand touched Fallon's shoulder. Kastambang said: "Master Antane, all is prepared. Will you come, pray?"

Fallon followed his host to a small room where two servants came forward, one with a mask and the other with a voluminous black robe."

"Don these," said Kastambang. "Your interlocutor will be similarly dight to forestall recognition."

Fallon, feeling foolishly histrionic, let the servants put the mask and robe upon him. Then Kastambang, puffing and hobbling, led him through passages hung with black velvet, which gave Fallon an uneasy feeling of passing down the alimentary canal of some great beast. They came to the door of another chamber, which the banker opened.

As he motioned Fallon in he said: "No tricks or violence, now. My men do guard all exits."

Then he went out and closed the door.

As Fallon's eyes surveyed the dim-lit chamber, the first thing that they encountered was a single, small oil-lamp burning in a niche before a writhesome, wicked-looking little copper god from far Ziada, beyond the Triple Seas. And against the opposite wall he saw a squat black shadow which suddenly shot up to a height equal to his own.

Fallon started, and his hand flew to his rapier-hilt—then he remembered that he had been relieved of his sword when he entered the house. Then he realized that the shadow was merely another man—or Krishnan—robed and hooded like himself.

"What wish you to know?" asked the black figure.

The voice was high with tension; the language was Balhibou; the accent—it sounded like that of eastern Balhib, where the tongue shaded into the westernmost varieties of Gozashtandou.

"The complete ritual of Yesht," said Fallon, fumbling for a pad and pencil and moving closer to the lamp.

"By the God of the Earthmen, 'tis no mean quest," said the other. "The enchiridion of prayers and hymns alone does occupy a weighty volume—I can remember but little of these."

"Is this enchiridion secret?"

"Nay. You can buy it at any good bookshop."

"Well then, give me everything that's *not* in the enchiridion: the costumes, movements, and so on."

An hour or so later, Fallon had the whole thing down in shorthand, nearly filling his pad. "Is that all there is?"

"All that I know of."

"Well, thanks a lot. You know, if I knew who you were, perhaps you and I could do one another a bit of good from time to time. I sometimes collect information . . ."

"For what purpose, good my sir?"

"Oh—let's say for stories for the *Rashm*." Fallon had actually supplied the paper with a few stories, which furnished a cover for his otherwise suspicious lack of regular employment.

The other said: "Without casting aspersions upon your goodwill, sir, I'm also aware that one who knew me and my history could, were he so minded, also wreak me grievous harm."

"No harm intended. After all I'd let you know who I was."

"I have more than a ghost of an idea," said the other. "A Terran from your twang, and I know that our host has bidden few such hither this night. A choosy wight."

Fallon thought of leaping upon the other and tearing off the mask. But then, he might get a knife in the ribs; and even unarmed, the fellow might be stronger than he. While the average Earthman, used to a slightly greater gravity, could out-wrestle the average Krishnan, that was not always true; besides Fallon was not so young as once.

"Very well," he said. "Good-bye." And he knocked on the

door by which he had entered.

As this door opened, Fallon heard his interlocutor knock likewise upon the other door. Fallon stepped out and followed the servant back through the velvet-hung passage to the room where he had received his disguise, which was here removed.

"Did you obtain satisfaction?" asked Kastambang, limping in. "Have you that which you sought?"

"Yes, thanks. May I ask what's the program for the rest of the evening."

"You're just in good time for the animal-battle."

"Oh?"

"Aye, aye. If you'll attend, I'll have a lackey show you to the basement. Attendance will be limited to males, firstly because we deem so sanguinary a spectacle unfit for the weaker sex, and secondly because so many of 'em have been converted by your Terran missionaries to the notion that such a spectacle is morally wrong. When our warriors become so effeminated that the sight of a little gore revolts 'em, then shall we deserve to fall beneath the shafts and scimitars of the Jungava."

"Surely, I'll go," said Fallon.

Kastambang's "basement" was an underground chamber the size of a small auditorium. Part of it was given over to a bar, gaming tables, and other amenities. The end, where the animal-fight was scheduled to occur, was hollowed out into a funnel-shaped depression ringed by several rows of seats and looking over the edge of a circular steep-sided pit a dozen or fifteen meters in diameter and about half as deep. The chamber was crowded with fifty or sixty male Krishnans. The air was thick with scent and smoke, and loud with talk in which each speaker tried to shout down all the others. Bets flew and drinks foamed.

As Fallon arrived, a couple of guests who had been arguing passed beyond the point of debate to that of action. One snapped his fingers at the other's nose, whereupon the second let the first have the contents of his stein in the face. The finger-snapper sputtered, screamed with rage, felt for his missing sword, and then flew upon his antagonist. In an instant they were rolling about the floor, kicking, clawing, and pulling each other's bushy green hair.

A squad of lackeys separated them, one nursing a bitten thumb and the other a fine set of facial scratches, and hustled them out by separate exits.

Fallon got a mug of kvad at the bar, greeted a couple of acquaintances, and wandered over to the pit, wither the rest of the company were also drifting. He thought: *I'll stay just long enough to see a little of this show, then push off for home.*

Mustn't let Kordaq and Gazi get back ahead of me.

By hurrying round to the farther side of the pit he managed to get one of the last front-row seats. As he leaned over the rail, he glanced to the sides and recognized his right-hand neighbor—a tall thin youngish ornately clad Krishnan, as Chindor er-Quinan, the leader of the secret opposition to mad King Kir.

Catching Chindor's eye he said: "Hello there, your Altitude."

"Hail, Master Antane. How wags your world?"

"Well enough, I suppose, though I haven't been back to it lately. What's on the program?"

" 'Twill be a yeki captured in the Forest of Jerab against a shan from the steaming jungles of Mutaabwk. Oh, know you my friend, Master Liyara the Brazer?"

"Delighted to meet you," said Fallon, grasping the proffered thumb and offering his own.

"And I to meet you," said Liyara. "It should be a spectacle rare, I ween. Would you make a small wager? I'll take the shan if you'll give odds."

"Even money on the yeki," said Fallon, staring.

The eastern accent was just like that which he had heard from the masked party. Was he mistaken, or had Liyara given him a rather keen look too?

"Dupulan take you!" said Liyara. "Three to two . . ."

The argument was interrupted by a movement and murmur in the audience, which had by now nearly all taken their seats. A tailed Koloftu popped out of a small door in the side of the pit, walked out to the middle of the arena, struck a small gong that he carried for silence, and announced:

"Gentle sirs, my master Kastambang proffers a beast-fight for your pleasure. From this portal . . ." (the hairy one gestured) "shall issue a full-grown male yeki from the forest of Jerab; while from yonder opening shall come a giant shan, captured at great risk in the equatorial jungles of Mutaabwk. Place your bets quickly, as the combat will begin as soon as we can drive the creatures forth. I thank your worships."

The Koloftu skipped out the way he had come. Liyara resumed: "Three to two, I said . . ."

But he was again interrupted by a grinding of gears and a rattle of chains, which announced that the barriers at the two larger portals were being raised. A deep roar reverberated up out of the arena, answered by a frightful snarl, as if a giant were tearing sheet-iron.

The roar came again, almost deafening, and out bounded a great brown furry carnivore: the yeki, looking something like a six-legged mink of tiger size. And out from the other entrance flowed an even more horrendous monster, also six-legged, but hairless and vaguely reptilian, with a longish neck and a body that tapered gradually down to a tail. Its leathery hide was brightly colored in a bewildering pattern of stripes and spots of deep green and buff. Fine camouflage for lurking in a thicket in tropical jungles, thought Fallon.

The land animals of Krishna had evolved from two separate aquatic stocks: one, oviparous, and four-legged, while the other was viviparous, and six-legged. The four-limbed subkingdom included the several humanoid species and a number of other forms including the tall camel-like shomal. The six-legged subkingdom took in many land forms such as the domesticable aya, shaihan, eshun, and bishtar; most of the carnivores; and the flying forms such as the aqebat, whose middle pair of limbs were developed into batlike wings. Convergent evolution had produced several striking parallels between the four-legged and the six-legged stocks, just as it had between the humanoid Krishnans and the completely unrelated Earthmen.

Fallon guessed that both beasts had been deliberately maltreated to rouse them to a pitch of fury. Their normal instinct would be to avoid each other.

The yeki crouched, sliding forward on its belly like a cat stalking a bird, its fangs bared in a continuous growl. The shan reared up, arching its neck into a swan-like curve, as it sidled around on its six taloned legs with a curious clockworky gait. Snarl after snarl came from its fang-bearing jaws. As the yeki came a little closer, the shan's head shot out and its jaws came together with a ringing snap—but the yeki, with the speed of thought, flinched back out of reach. Then it began its creeping advance again.

The Krishnans were working themselves into a state of the wildest excitement. They shouted bets at each other clear across the pit. They leaped up and down in their seats like monkeys and screamed to those in front to sit down. Beside Fallon, Chindor er-Qinan was tearing his elegant bonnet to pieces.

Snap-snap-snap went the great jaws. The whole audience gave a deafening yell at the first sight of blood. The yeki had not dodged the shan's lunge quickly enough, and the tropical carnivore's teeth had gashed its antagonist's shoulder. Brown blood, like cocoa, oozed down the yeki's glossy fur.

A few seats away, a Krishnan was trying to make a bet with Chindor, but neither could make himself heard above the din. At last the Krishnan nobleman stumbled over Fallon's knees and into the aisle. Then he climbed to where his interlocutor was shouting his odds between cupped hands. Others in the rear had climbed over the seats to stand behind those in the front row, peering over their shoulders.

Snap-snap! More blood; both yeki and shan were cut. The air reeked of cigar-smoke, strong perfume, alcohol, and the body-odors of the Krishnans and the beasts below. Fallon coughed. Liyara the Brazer was shrieking something.

The foaming jaws approached each other, each of the animals watching the other for the first move. Fallon found himself gripping the rail with knuckle-whitening force.

Crunch! The shan and the yeki struck together. The shan seized the yeki's foreleg, but the yeki at the same instant clamped its jaws upon the shan's neck. In an instant, the sand of the pit flew as the two rolled over, thrashing and clawing. The whole mansion shook as the massive limbs and bodies slammed against the wooden walls of the pit with drumlike booming sounds.

Fallon, like the rest of the audience, had his eyes so closely glued to the beasts that he was unaware of his surroundings—until he felt the grip of a pair of powerful hands upon his ankles, lifting. One heave and over the rail he went, plunging downward toward the sand.

He had a flashing impression that Liyara had thrown him over; then the sand smote him in the face with stunning force.

Fallon rolled over, feeling as if his neck had been broken. It was, as he found by moving, merely wrenched. He scrambled up to face the yeki, which stood over the shan. The latter was plainly dead.

He glanced up. A ring of pale-green faces stared down upon him. Most of them had their mouths open, but he could not make out anything, because they were all shouting at once.

"A sword!" he yelled. "Somebody throw me a sword!"

There was a commotion among the audience. Nobody had any swords, as they all had been left in the cloak-room on arrival. Somebody called for a rope, somebody else for a ladder, and somebody else shouted something about knotting coats together. They milled around, screaming advice but accomplishing nothing.

The yeki began to slither forward on its belly.

And then the master of the house himself leaned over the railing, shouting: "*Ohe,* Master Antane! Catch!"

Down came a sword, hilt first. Fallon leaped and caught the hilt, spun, and faced the yeki.

The beast was still advancing. In an instant, Fallon surmised, it would spring or rush, and then his sword would be of no use. He might, with luck, deal it a mortal stab; but much good that would do him—he could still be slain by the dying monster.

The only defense would be a strong offense. Fallon advanced upon the yeki, sword out. The creature roared and slashed out with its unwounded foreleg. Fallon flicked out his blade and scratched the clawed paw.

The yeki roared more loudly. Fallon, heart pounding, drove his point at the beast's nose. At the first prick, the yeki backed up, snarling and foaming.

"Master Antane!" shouted a voice. "Drive it toward the open portal!"

Thrust; gain a step; thrust again; jerk the sword back as the great paw slapped at it. Another step. Little by little, Fallon herded the yeki toward the portal, every minute expecting it to spring in its fury and finish him.

Then, aware of sanctuary, the beast abruptly turned and slithered snakelike into the cavernous opening in the wall. With a flash of brown fur it was gone. The gate clanged down.

Fallon reeled. At last somebody lowered a ladder. He climbed up slowly, and handed the sword back to Kastambang.

Hands pounded Fallon's back; hands pressed cigars and drinks upon him; hands hoisted him on to Krishnan shoulders and marched him around the room. There was nothing reserved about Krishnans. The climax came when one of them handed Fallon a hatful of gold and silver pieces which he had collected among the company as a tribute to the gallantry of the Earthman.

There was no sign of Liyara. From the remarks passed, Fallon guessed that nobody had seen the manufacturer throw him over the rail:

"By the nose of Tyazan, why fell you in?" "Had you one too many?" "Nay, he slays monsters for pleasure!"

If, now, Fallon burst into accusation there would be only his word against Liyara's.

Several hours, and many drinks, later, Fallon found himself lolling in a khizun with a couple of fellow-guests, roaring a drunken song to the six-beat clop of the aya's feet. The others got out before he did, as none lived so far into the poorer districts to the west. This would mean his paying the others' fare as well as his own. But with all that money that they had collected for him . . .

Where in Hishkak was it, anyhow? Then he remembered a series of wild crap-games that at one point had him rich to the tune of thirty thousand karda. But then fickle Da'vi, the Varasto goddess of luck, deserted him, and soon he was down to just the money that he had brought with him to Kastambang's house.

He groaned. Would he never learn? With the small fortune that he had had in his grip, he could have shaken the dust of dusty Balhib from his boots, leaving Mjipa and Qais and Fredro to solve the secret of the Safq as best they could, and hired mercenaries in Majbur to retake Zamba.

And now, another horrid thought struck him. What with the adventure with the yeki, and his subsequent orgy of relaxation, he had lost track of time and forgotten all about Gazi and her engagement with Kordaq. Surely they would be back by now—and what excuse should he offer? He clutched his aching head. He no doubt stank like a distillery. In the last analysis, of course, one could fall back upon the truth.

His mind, usually so fertile in excuses and expedients, seemed paralyzed. Let's see: "My friends Gargan and Weems dropped in to see how I was; and I felt so much better that they persuaded me to go round to Savaich's with them, and there my stomach went dobby-o again . . ."

She wouldn't believe it, but it was the best that he could do in his present state. The khizun drew up at his door. As he paid his fare his eyes roamed the exiguous façade, which looked less loathsome in the moonlight than by day. There was no sign of light. Either Gazi was in bed, or . . .

As Fallon let himself in, a feeling told him that the house was empty. And so it proved; nor was there any note from Gazi.

He stumbled up the stairs, pulled off his sword and boots, threw himself across the bed, and fell into troubled slumber.

Chapter X

Anthony Fallon awakened stiff and uncomfortable, with a vile taste in his mouth. His neck felt as if it had acquired a permanent kink from last night's fall. Gradually, as he pulled himself together, he remembered finding Gazi not yet returned . . .

Where was she now?

He sat up, and called. No answer.

Fallon sat on the edge of the bed for a few seconds, rubbing the sleep out of his eyes and jerking his head this way and that to exercise his wrenched neck. Then he got up and searched the house. Still no Gazi. Not only was she gone; she had taken her clothes and minor possessions with her.

As he prepared breakfast with shaking hands, his mind wandered over the various possibilities. Fallon might have reflected that, after all, in Balhib, women were free to change their jagains whenever they pleased. But just now, the mere thought that Gazi might have deserted him for Kordaq roused such rage as to sweep all other considerations aside.

He choked down a cold breakfast, pulled on his boots, hitched up his sword and, without bothering to shave, set out for the barracks at the east side of the town. The sun had been up less than a Krishnan hour, and the breeze was beginning to make the dust-whirls dance.

A half-hour's ride on the aya-drawn bus brought him to the barracks, where a surly soldier at the reception desk gave him the address of Kordaq's suite of rooms. Another half-hour brought his search to a close.

The apartment house which Kordaq lived in stood at the northern end of the Kharju, where the shops and banks of that district gave way to the middle-class residences of the Zardu to the north. Fallon read the names of the tenants on the plaque affixed to the wall beside the door, and stamped up the stairs to the third floor. He made sure of the right door and struck the gong beside it.

When there was no response, he struck it again, harder, and finally knocked on the door, which the Balhibuma seldom did. At length he heard movement inside, and the door opened to reveal an extremely sleepy and confused-looking Kordaq. His green hair was awry; a blanket protected his bony shoulders against the early-morning chill, and he carried a naked sword in his hand. It was normal for a Krishnan thus to answer a knock at so untoward an hour, for Fallon might as well have been a robber.

Kordaq asked, "What in the name of Hoi's green eyes—oh, 'tis Master Antane! what brings you hither to shatter my slumber, sir? Some gross emergency dire, I trust?"

"Where's Gazi?" said Fallon, his hand straying behind him toward his own hilt.

Kordaq blinked some more sleep out of his eyes. "Why," he replied innocently, "having done me the honor to take me as her new jagain—in consequence of your folly of yester-eve, whereby, despite all I could do, your deception of her revealed itself—the girl's with me. Where else?"

"You . . . you mean you admit . . ."

"Admit what? I'm telling you straight. Now get you hence, good my sir, and let me resume my disjoined doze. Next time, I pray, call upon a night-working man at some more seemly hour."

Fallon choked with rage. "You think you can walk off with my woman, and then tell me to go away and let you sleep?"

"What ails you, Earthman? This is not barbarous Qaath, where women are property. Now get out, ere I teach you a lesson in manners . . ."

"Oh, yes?" snarled Fallon. "I'll teach you a manner!"

He stepped back, whipped out his sword in a behind-the-back

draw, and bored in.

Still somewhat fogged with sleep, Kordaq hesitated for a fraction of a second before deciding whether to meet the attack or to slam the door shut; thus, Fallon's blade was lunging toward his chest before he moved. By a hasty parry, combined with a backwards leap, he barely saved himself from being spitted.

In so doing, however, he relinquished control over the door; Fallon plunged through and kicked the door shut behind him.

"Madman!" said Kordaq, whipping off his blanket and whirling it around his right arm for a shield. "Your imminent doom's upon your own head." And he rushed in his turn.

Tick-zing-clang went the heavy blades. Fallon beat off the attack, but his ripostes and counters were stopped with ease by Kordaq, either with his blade or with his blanketed arm. Fallon was too full of the urge to kill to notice what an odd spectacle his opponent made, nude but for the sword and the blanket.

"Antane!" cried Gazi's voice.

Fallon and Kordaq both let their eyes stray for a fleeting instant toward the door, in which Gazi stood with her hands pressed to her cheeks. But instantly each brought back his attention to his opponent before the other could take advantage of the distraction.

Tsing-click-swish!

The fighters circled, warier now. Fallon knew from the first few passages that they were well matched. While he was heavier and (being an Earthman) basically stronger, Kordaq was younger and had the longer reach. Kordaq's blanket offset Fallon's superior fencing-technique.

Tick-tick-clang!

Fallon knocked over a small table, kicked it out of the way.

Swish-chunk!

Kordaq feinted, then aimed a vicious cut at Fallon's head. Fallon ducked; the slash sheared through the bronze stem of the floor-lamp and set its top bouncing across the floor, while the remainder of the standard toppled over with a crash.

Clang-dzing!

Round and round they went. Once when Fallon found himself facing Gazi in the doorway, he took the occasion to shout, "I say, Gazi, go away! You're distracting us!"

She paid no attention, and the duel continued. By a sudden flurry of thrusts and lunges Kordaq backed Fallon against a wall. A final lunge would have nailed him to the wall, but Fallon jumped aside and Kordaq's point pierced the room's one picture, a cheap copy of Ma'shir's well-known painting *Dawn Over Majbur*. While Kordaq's blade was stuck in the plaster, Fallon gave a quick forehand cut at his foe, who caught the blow on his blanket, jerked out his sword, and faced his opponent again.

Tink-swish!

Fallon threw another cut at Kordaq, who parried slantwise so that Fallon's blade bit into the little overturned table.

Fallon felt his blood pound in his ears. He moved slowly, it seemed to him as if wading through tar. But Kordaq, he could see, was getting just as tired.

Tick-clank!

The fight went on and on until both fighters were so exhausted that they could do little more than stand on guard, glaring at one another. Every ten seconds or so one or the other would summon up energy to make a feint or a lunge, which the other's unpierceable defense always stopped.

Ding-zang!

Fallon grated, "We're too—damned even!"

Gazi's voice proclaimed, "What ails you is that you're both cowards at liver, fearing to close each upon the other."

Kordaq shouted in a strangled voice, "Madam, would you like to trade places with me—to see how easy this is?"

"You are ridiculous," said Gazi. "I thought one or the other would be slain, so that my problem should be solved by choosing the survivor. But if you'll merely caper and mow all day . . ."

Fallon panted, "Kordaq, I think—she's urging us on—so she can enjoy—the sight of gore—at our expense."

"Methinks—you speak sooth—Master Antane."

They puffed for a few seconds more, like a pair of idling steam-locomotives. Then Fallon said, "Well, how about calling it off? It doesn't look—as if either of us—could best the other in a fair fight."

"You started it, sir, but if you wish to terminate it, I—as a reasonable man—will gladly entertain the proposal."

"So moved."

Fallon stepped back and half-sheathed his sword, watching Kordaq against any treacherous attack. Kordaq stepped into the alcove inside the door and sheathed his sword in the empty scabbard that hung from one of the coat-hooks. He looked at Fallon to be sure that the latter's blade was all the way in and his hand was off the hilt before he released his own hilt. Then he carried sword and scabbard toward the bedroom.

Before he reached the entrance, Gazi turned her back and preceded him. Fallon fell into a chair. From the bedroom came sounds of recrimination. Then Gazi reappeared in shawl, skirt, and sandals, lugging a cloth bag containing her gear. Behind her came Kordaq, also clad and buckling on his scabbard.

"Men," said Gazi, "whether Krishnan or Terran, are the most sorry, loathly, despicable, fribbling creatures in the animal kingdom. Seek not to find me, either of you, for I'm through with you both. Farewell and good riddance!"

She slammed the door behind her. Kordaq laughed and dropped into another chair, sprawling exhaustedly.

"That was my hardiest battle since I fought the Jungava at Tajrosh," he said. "I wonder what raised up yon wench's ire so. She boiled up like a summer thunder-shower over Qe'ba's crags."

Fallon shrugged. "Sometimes I doubt if I understand females either."

"Have you breakfasted?"

"Yes."

"Ha, that explains your success. Had I fought upon a stomach full, 'twould have been another story. Come into the kitchen whilst I scramble a deye egg."

Fallon grunted and got to his feet. He found Kordaq assembling comestibles from the shelves of the kitchen, including a big jug of falat-wine.

"'Tis a trifle early in the day to start on kvad," said the captain, "but fighting's a thirsty game, and a drop of this to replace that which we've sweated forth will harm us not."

Several mugs of wine later, Fallon, feeling mellow, said, "Kordaq old fellow, I can't tell you how glad I am you didn't get hurt. You're my idea of what a man should be."

"Forsooth, friend Antane, my sentiments toward you exactly. I'd rate you even with my dearest friends of my own species, than which I know of no more liver-felt compliment."

"Let's drink to friendship."

"Hail friendship!" cried Kordaq, raising his mug.

"To stand or fall together!" said Fallon.

Kordaq, having drunk, set down his mug and looked sharply at Fallon. "Speaking of which, my good bawcock, as you seem—when not inflamed by barbarous jealousy—to be a wight of sense and discretion, and serve under me in the Guard, I feel I should cast a hint of warning in your direction, to do with as you will."

"What's this?"

"The news is that the barbarian conqueror, Ghuur of Qaath, marches at last. Word arrived by bijar-post yester-eve shortly ere I left the barracks to visit your house. He had not then yet crossed the frontier, but news of that impious introgression may have come by now."

"I suppose that means that the Guard . . . ?"

"You divine my very thought, sir. Get your affairs in order, as you may be called out any day. And now I must report to the barracks, to spend the day, no doubt, composing commands and filling forms. Another horrid institution! Would I'd been born some centuries back, when the art of writing was so rare that soldiers carried all they needed to know in their heads."

"Who'll guard the city if the whole Guard's called out?"

"They'll not all be summoned. The probationaries, the incapacitated, and the retired members shall remain to fill the duties of those who leave. We captains of the watch-companies do struggle with the minister, who wishes to keep hale and blooming guardsmen for special watch-duty in . . ."

"In the Safq?" asked Fallon as Kordaq hesitated.

The captain belched. "I'd not so state, save that you seem apprised of this circumstance already. How heard you?"

"Oh, you know. Rumors. But what's *in* the thing?"

"That I truly may not divulge. I'll say this: that this ancient pile harbors something so new and deadly as to make the shafts of Ghuur's bowmen seem harmless as a vernal shower."

Fallon said, "The Yeshtites have certainly done an amazing job of keeping the interior of the Safq secret. I don't know of a single plan of the place in circulation."

Kordaq smiled and wiggled one antenna in the Krishnan equivalent of a wink. "Not so secret as they like to think. This mystery has leaked a bit, as such mummeries are wont to do."

"You mean somebody outside the cult does know?"

"Aye, sir. Or at least we have a suspicion." Kordaq drank down another mug of falat-wine.

"Who's 'we'?"

"A learned fraternity whereto I belong, yclept the Mejraf Janjira. Hast heard of us?"

"The Neophilosophical Society," murmured Fallon. "I know a little about their tenets. You mean that *you* . . ." Fallon checked himself in time to keep from saying that he deemed these tenets an egregious example of interstellar damnfoolishness.

Kordaq, however, caught the scorn in the closing words and looked severely at Fallon. "There are those who condemn our principles unheard, proving thereby their ignorance in rejecting wisdom without making fair trial thereof. Now, I'll explain them in three words, as best I can in my poor tongue-tied fashion—and if you're interested I can refer you to others more adept in exposition than I. Hast heard of Pyatsmif?"

"Of *what?*"

"Pyatsmif . . . That proves the ignorance of Earthmen, who have not heard of some of their planet's greatest men."

"You mean that's an Earthman?" Fallon had never heard of Charles Piazzi Smith, the eccentric Scottish nineteenth-century astronomer who founded the pseudo-scientific cult of pyramidology; but even if he had, it is doubtful whether he would have recognized the name as Kordaq pronounced it.

"Well," said the captain, "this Pyatsmif was the first to realize that a great and ancient monument upon your planet's face —ancient, that is, as upstart Terrans reckon age—was more than it seemed. Truly, it incorporated in its moldering structure clues to the wisdom of ages and the secrets of the universe . . ."

For the next half-hour Fallon squirmed while Kordaq lectured. He did not dare to break off the audience, because he thought that Kordaq might have some useful information.

At the end of that time, however, the falat-wine was having a definite effect upon the captain's discourse, causing him to ramble and to lose the thread of his argument.

He finally got himself so confused that he broke off: ". . . nay, good Antane, I'm a simple tashiturn soldier, no ph'los'pher. Had I the eloquence of . . . of . . ."

He broke off, staring blankly into space. Fallon said, "And you've got a plan of the Safq?"

Kordaq looked fuzzily sly. "Sh-said I so? Methinks I did not. But that such a plan exists I'll not deny."

"Interesting if true."

"Doubt you my word, sirrah? I am who I am . . ."

"Now, now. I'll believe your plan when I see it. There's no law against that, is there?"

"No law against . . ." Kordaq puzzled over this problem for a while, then shook his head as if to clear it. "As stubborn as a bishtar and as slippery as a fondaq, such is my copemate Antane. Very well, I'll *show* you this plan, or a copy true thereof. Then will you believe?"

"Oh, ah, yes, I suppose so."

Kordaq swaying, went into the living room. Fallon heard the sound of drawers opening and closing, and the captain came back with a piece of Krishnan paper in his hand. "Here then!" he said, and spread it out upon the table.

Fallon saw that it bore a rough diagram of the ground-floor plan of the Safq, which he could recognize by its curiously curved outline. The drawing was not very clear because it had been made with a Krishnan lead-pencil. This meant that it had a "lead" of real metallic lead, not of graphite, a comparatively rare mineral on this planet.

Fallon pointed to the largest room shown in the plan, just inside the only doorway. "That, I suppose, is the main temple or chapel?"

"Truly I know not, for I've never been inside to see. But your hypothesis seems to accord with the divine faculty of reason, good sir."

The rest of the plan showed a maze of rooms and corridors, which meant little unless one knew the purposes of each part or had visited the site. Fallon stared at the plan with all his might, trying to photograph it on his brain. "Where did this come from?"

"Oh, ha, 'twas a frolicksome tale. A member of our learned brotherhood by inadvertence got into the secret annex of the royal library, where the public's not allowed, and came upon a whole file of such plans, showing all the important buildings in Balhib. He said nought at the time, but as soon as he was out of this hole he drew a copy from memory, of which this is yet another copy."

The captain put the paper away, saying: "And now if you'll excuse me, dear comrade, I must to toil. Qarar's blood! I've drunk too much of that belly-wash and must needs walk to work to sober up. Lord Chindor would take it amiss, did I enter the barracks staggering like a drunken Osirian and falling over the furniture. Wilt walk with me?"

"Gladly," said Fallon, and followed Kordaq out.

Chapter XI

"What is?" asked Dr. Julian Fredro.

Fallon explained. "Everything's ready for our invasion of the Safq. I've even got a plan of the ground floor. Here!"

He showed Fredro the plan that he had drawn from memory, as soon as he had bidden farewell to Kordaq and had acquired a pencil and a pad of paper at a shop in the Kharju.

"Good, good," said Fredro. "When is this to be?"

"Tomorrow night. But you'll have to come with me now to order your costume."

Fredro looked doubtful. "I am writing important report for *Przeglad Archeologiczny* . . ."

Fallon held up a hand. "That'll wait—this won't. It'll take my tailor the rest of the day to make the robes. Besides, tomorrow's is the only Full Rite of Yesht for three ten-nights. Something to do with astrological conjunctions. And the Full Rite is the only one where they have such a crowd of priests that we could slip in among them unnoticed. So it'll have to be tomorrow night."

"Oh, very well. Wait till I get coat."

They left the 'Avrud Terrao, or Terran Hotel, and walked to the shop of Ve'qir the Exclusive. Fallon got Ve'qir aside and asked, "You're a Bakhite, aren't you?"

"Aye, Master Antane. Wherefore ask you?"

"I wanted to be sure you wouldn't have religious objections to filling my order."

"By Qarar's club, sir, 'tis an ominous note you sound! What order's this?"

"Two robes of priests of Yesht, third grade . . ."

"Why, have you gentiles been admitted to that priesthood?"

"No, but we want them anyway."

"Oh, sir! Should it become known, I have many customers among the Yeshtites . . ."

"It shan't become known. But you'll have to make them with your own hands, and we have to have them right away, too."

The couturier grumped and fussed and squirmed, but Fallon finally talked him round.

Most of the morning was spent in the back room of the shop being measured and fitted. This proved not too difficult, as the loose tentlike robes which the cult of Yesht decreed for its priesthood had to fit only approximately. Ve'qir promised the garments by the following noon, so Fallon and Fredro separated, the latter to return to the 'Avrud Terrao to resume work on his article.

Fallon said in parting, "You'll have to get rid of those whiskers too, old man."

"Shave my little beard? Never! Have worn this beard on five different planets! I have right to wear . . ."

Fallon shrugged. "Suit yourself, but you can't pass as a Krishnan then. They've got hardly any hair on their faces."

Fredro grumpily gave in, and they agreed to meet the following morning, pick up the robes, and go to Fallon's house to rehearse the ritual.

Fallon went thoughtfully back to the Juru, had lunch, and returned home. As he neared his house he observed a little wooden arrow hanging by a string from the doorknob.

With a grunt of displeasure, Fallon lifted the object off its support. This meant that there would be a meeting of all members of the Juru Company at the armory that evening. No doubt this meeting was connected with the rising peril of Qaath.

Captain Kordaq faced the assembled Juru Company—two hundred and seventeen organisms. About half were Krishnans; the rest were Earthmen, Thothians, Osirians, and so on.

He cleared his throat and said, "You've no doubt heard the rumors that have been buzzing around the Qaathian question like chidebs about a ripe cadaver, and have surmised that you've been called hither on that account. I'll not deceive you—you have. And though I'm but a rude and taciturn soldier, I'll essay to set before you in three words the causes thereof.

"As you all know—and as some of you recall from personal and painsome experience—'twas but seven years ago that the Kamuran of Qaath (may Dupulan bury him in filth) smote us at Tajrosh and scattered our warriors to the winds. This battle bereft us of mastery of the Pandrate of Jo'ol, which theretofore had stood as a buffer 'twixt us and the wild men of the steppes. Ghuur's mounted archers swarmed all over that land like a plague of zi'dams, and Ghuur himself received the homage of the Pandr of Jo'ol, who in sooth could do little else. Since then Jo'ol has remained independent in name, but its Pardr looks to Ghuur of Uriiq for protection 'stead of to our own government."

"If we had a king in his right mind . . ." somebody said from the back, but the interrupter was quickly shushed.

"There shall be no disrespect for the royal house," said Kordaq sternly. "While I, too, am aware of his Altitude's tragic indisposition, yet the monarchy—and not the man—is what we owe allegiance to. To continue: Since then, mighty Ghuur has spread his pestilent power, subduing Dhaukia and Suria and adding them to his ever-growing empire. His cavalry have borne their victorious arms to the stony Madhiq Mountains, to the marshes of Lake Khaast, and even to the unknown lands of Ghobbejd and Yeramis—hitherto little more to us than names on the edge of the map, tenanted by headless men and polymorphic monsters.

"Why, you may well ask, did he not smite Balhib before sending his banner into such distant territories? Because, though we may have degenerated from our greatest days, we're still a martial race, tempered like steel betwixt the hammer of the Jungava and the anvil of the other Varasto nations, to whom we've served these many centuries as a shield against the inroads of the steppe-folk. And though Ghuur vanquished us at Tajrosh, he was so mauled in the doing that he lacked force to push across the border into Balhib proper.

"Now, having bound many nations to his chariot, the barbarian has at last collected force enough to try hand-strokes with us again. His armies have swept into unresisting Jo'ol. Any hour we may hear that they have crossed our border. Scouts report that they are as grains of sand for multitude—that their shafts blacken the sun and their soldiery drink the rivers dry. Besides the dreaded mounted archery of Qaath, there are footmen from Suria, dragoons from Dhaukia, longbowmen from Madhiq, and men of far fantastic tribes in sunset lands never heard of among the Varastuma. And rumors speak of novel instruments of war, ne'er before seen upon this planet.

"Do I tell you this to affright you? Nay. For we, too, have our strength. I need not recite to you the past glories of Balhibo arms." (Kordaq reeled off a long list of events unnecessary to mention.)

"But besides our own strong left arms we have something new. 'Tis a weapon of such fell puissance that a herd of wild bishtars could not stand before it! If all goes well 'twill be ready by Fiveday's drill—three days hence. Prepare yourselves for stirring action!

"Now, another matter, my chicks. The Juru Company's notorious in Zanid's guard for lack of uniform—wherefor you're not to be blamed. By your weird diversity of form you defeat the very purpose of a uniform. However, some measure must be taken, lest you find yourselves upon the field of furious battle without means of telling friend from foe, and so be swallowed in confusion and swept into ill-deserved oblivion by your own side's ignorant arms, as happened to Sir Zidzuresh in the legend.

"I've searched the arsenal and found this pile of ancient helms. 'Tis true they're badly scarred by the subtle demon of rust, albeit the armorers have ground and scoured them to oust the worst corrosion. But at least they're all of a pattern, and in want of other means of identification they'll distinguish the heroes of the Juru as well as protect your skulls.

"In addition, the proper uniform of the Juru Company—as well you know—comprises a red jacket with one white band sewn to the right sleeve, and not these trifling brassards you wear on patrol. Therefore if any of you has aught in his closet that could serve this vital turn, let him bring it forth. Its cut matters little, so that it be red. Then set you your sisters and jagainis to sewing white bands upon the sleeves. No petty foppery is this—your lives may hang upon your diligence in giving substance to this command!

"One more matter, also a thing of weight and moment. It's come to the governments's keen and multitudinous ears that agents of the accursed Ghuur do slink like spooks about our sacred city. Guard, then, your tongues, and watch lest any fellow citizen display unwonted curiosity in manners of no just concern to him! If we catch one of these rascals in his slimy turpitudes, his fate shall make the historian's pen to shake and the reader thereof to shudder in generations to come!

"Now form a line for the fitting and distribution of these antique sconces, and may you wear them like the heroes stout who bore them in the great days of yore!"

As he lined up to get his helmet, Fallon reflected that Kordaq had not been very discreet himself that morning. It also occurred to him what a fine joke it would be if he, Anthony Fallon, were killed because of some of the information that he had sold to the opposing side.

Fallon was lured into Savaich's on his way home, and spent hours there talking and drinking with his cronies. Therefore he again slept late the following morning and hastened to cross the city to pick up Fredro at the Terrao.

It seemed to him that a subtle excitement ran through the city. On the omnibus, he caught snatches of conversation about the new events:

". . . aye, sir, 'tis said the Jungava have a force of bishtars, twice the size of ours, which can be driven in wild stampede through the lines of their foes . . ." "Methinks our generals are fools, to send our boys off to the distant prairies to fight. 'Twere better to wait until the foe's here, and meet them upon our own ground . . ." "All this stir and armament is but a provocation to Ghuur of Uriiq. Did we but remain tranquil, sir, he'd never bethink himself of us . . ." "Nay, 'tis a weak and degenerate age, sir. In our grandsires' time we'd have spat in the barbarian's face . . ."

Fallon found the archeologist typing on his little portable an article in his native language, which, as Fallon glanced over his shoulder, seemed to consist mainly of z's, j's, and w's. Fredro's chin and lip were still adorned with the mustache and goatee, which he had simply forgotten to remove.

Fallon nagged his man until the latter came out of his fog, and they walked to the shop of Ve'qir the Exclusive. After an hour's wait they set out, with their robes in a bundle under Fredro's arm, for Fallon's home. The omnibus was clopping past Zanid's main park, south of the House of Judgment between the Gabanj and the Bacha, when Fredro gripped Fallon's arm and pointed.

"Look!" he cried. "Is zoölogical garden!"

"Well?" said Fallon. "I know it."

"But I do not! Have not seen! Let us get off, yes? We can look at animals and have the lunch there."

Without waiting for Fallon to argue, the Pole leaped up from his seat and plunged down the stairs to the rear of the vehicle. Fallon followed, dubiously.

Presently they were wandering past cages containing yekis, shaihans, karouns, bishtars, and other denizens of the Krishnan wilds. Fredro asked, "What is crowd? Must be a something unusual."

A mass of Krishnans had collected in front of a cage. In the noon heat most of them had discarded shawls and tunics and were nude but for loincloths or skirts and footgear. The Earthmen walked toward them. They could not see what was in the cage for the mass of people, but over the heads of these an extra-large sign was fastened to the bars. Fallon, with effort, translated:

> BLAK BER; URSO NEGRO
> Habitat: Yunaisteits, Nortamerika, Terra

"Oh," said Fallon. "I remember *him*. I wrote the story in the *Rashm* when he arrived as a cub. He's Kir's pride and joy. Kir wanted to bring an elephant from Earth, but the freight on even a baby elephant was too much for the treasury."

"But what *is?*"

"An American black bear. If you want to elbow through this crowd to look at one fat, sleepy, and perfectly ordinary bear . . ."

"I see, I see. Let us look at the other things."

They were hanging over the edge of the avval tank, and watching the ten-meter crocodile-snakes swimming back and forth in it—one end of a given avval would be swimming back while the other was swimming forth—when a skirling sound made itself evident.

Fallon looked around and said, "Oy! Watch out—here comes the king! Damn—I should have remembered he comes here almost daily to feed the animals!"

Fredro paid no attention, being absorbed in extracting from his right eye a speck of dust that the wind had wafted into it.

Chapter XII

The sound of the royal pipers and drummer grew louder, and presently the whole procession swung into sight around a bend in one of the paths. First came the three pipers and the drummer. The pipers blew on instruments something like Scottish bagpipes but more complicated; the drummer beat a pair of copper kettle-drums. After them came six tall guards in gilded cuirasses, two with ivory-inlaid crossbows over their shoulders, two with halberds, and two with great two-handed swords.

In the midst of them walked a very tall Krishnan of advanced years, helping himself along with a jewelled walkingstick. He was dressed in garments of considerable magnificence, but put on all awry. His stocking-cap turban was loosely wound; his gold-embroidered jacket had the laces tangled; and his boots did not match. Behind the guards trailed a half-dozen miscellaneous civilians, their clothes rippling in the breeze.

The crowd of Krishnans around the bear-cage had dispersed at the first sound of the pipes. Now there were only a few Krishnans in sight, and these were sinking to one knee.

Fallon yanked Fredro's arm. "Kneel down, you damned fool!"

"What?" Fredro looked out of a red and watery eye from which he had at last dislodged the foreign particle. "Me kneel? I am citizen of P-Polish Republic, good as anybody else . . ."

Fallon half drew his rapier. "You kneel, old boy, or I'll bloody well let some of the stuffing out of you!"

Grumbling, Fredro complied. But, as the band went past, the tall, eccentrically clad Krishnan said something sharp. The procession halted. King Kir was staring fixedly at the face of Dr. Julian Fredro, who imperturbably returned the stare.

"So!" cried the king at last. " 'Tis the cursed Shurgez, come back to mock me! And wearing my stolen beard, I'll be bound! I'll trounce the pugging pajock in seemly style!"

Instantly the gaggle of trailing civilians began to close in around the king, all chattering soothing statements at once. Kir, paying them no heed, grasped his staff in both hands and tugged. It transpired that this was a sword-cane. Out came the sword, and the Dour of Balhib rushed at Fredro, point first.

"Run!" yelled Fallon, doing so without waiting to see if Fredro had the sense to follow.

At the first bend in the path, Fallon risked a glance to the rear. Fredro was several paces behind him. After him came Kir; and after the king came pipers, drummer, guards, and keepers strung out along the path and all shouting advice as to how to subdue the mad monarch without committing *lèse majesté*.

Fallon ran on. He had been to the zoo only twice during his stay in Zanid and so did not know the ground plan well. Hence when he came to an intersection, and the path ahead seemed to lead between two cages, he kept right on going.

Too late, he realized that this was a service-path leading to a locked door in each of the flanking cages; beyond that point, the path ceased. The ground sloped sharply up to a rocky crag that formed the back of both inclosures. One could climb up this slope a few meters only before it became too steep for further ascent. At the topmost point that could be reached, the bars of qong-wood that formed the cage stood only about two meters high, as the slope of the rock inside the cage at this point was too steep for the inmates of the cage to scale.

Fallon looked back. Despite his age, Fredro was still close behind him. King Kir was just galloping into the service-way with gleaming blade. There was no way to go but up the slope.

Up Fallon went until he was using his hands. Where a hint

of a ledge provided a toe-hold he looked down. Fredro was right below him, and the king was just starting to climb, while the royal retinue ran after and a horde of shouting spectators converged from all quarters. Fallon could of course have drawn his own sword and beaten off the king's attack; but had he done so, the guards—seeing him in combat with their demented lord—would have plugged him on general principles.

The only way out seemed at this point to be over the fence and into one of the cages. Fallon had not had time to read the signs on the fronts of the cages, and from where he now stood he could see only the backs of these signs. The right-hand cage held a pair of gerkas, medium-sized carnivores related to the larger yeki. These might well prove dangerous if their cage were invaded by strangers. Whatever was in the left-hand cage, it was at the moment withdrawn into its cave at the back.

Fallon grasped the tops of the bars on the left and heaved himself up. Though he was getting on in years, the less-than-Terran gravity, plus the fear of death, enabled him to hoist himself to the top of the fence, which he straddled. He held out a hand to the panting Fredro who, he noticed, still clutched the bundle containing the priestly robes. Fredro passed this bundle to Fallon, who dropped it on the inside of the fence. The bundle struck the nearly level rock at the base of the fence, then tipped over the edge and slid down the smooth slope until it stopped at a ledge.

With Fallon's help, Fredro also hauled himself to the top, then dropped down inside just as King Kir appeared outside the bars. Clutching a cage-bar to keep himself from slipping, the Dour thrust his sword between the bars.

As the blade flicked out, the two Earthmen slid off down the slope as the bundle had done, stopping on the same ledge. Here Fredro collapsed in a heap from exhaustion.

Behind them rose the yell of the mad monarch: "Come back, ye thievish slabberers, and receive your just guerdon!"

The retinue, having sorted itself out from the mere spectators, was climbing up after their king. As Fallon watched, they surrounded Kir, soothing and flattering, until presently the whole crowd was climbing back down the slope and walking out from between the two cages. The guards shooed the curious out of the way and the royal party set off, the pipers tootling again and the king completely surrounded by keepers.

"Now if we can only get out . . ." said Fallon, looking around for a path.

The rock was too steep and slippery to climb up the way they had come down; but at one end, the ledge ran into a mass of irregular rock that provided means of descent to a point from which it should be an easy jump to the floor of the inclosure.

A little knot of park officials had collected at the front of the cage, and seemed to be arguing the proper method of disposing of their unintended captives, gesticulating at one another with Latin verve. Around and behind them the crowd of spectators had closed in again following the passage of the king.

Fredro, having gotten his wind back and recovered from his unwonted exertions, rose, picked up the bundle, and started along the ledge, saying, "Not good—not good if this was found, yes?" He panted some more. Then: "What—ah—what does 'shurgez' mean, Mr. Fallon? The king shouted it at me again and again."

"Shurgez was a knight from Mikardand who cut off Kir's beard, so our balmy king has been sensitive on the subject ever since. It never occurred to me that that little goatee of yours would set him off— I say, look who's here!"

A thunderous snarl made both men recoil back against the rock. Out from the cave at the back of the cage, its six lizardy legs moving like clockwork, came the biggest shan that Fallon had even seen. The saucer eyes picked out Fallon and Fredro on their ledge.

Fredro cried, "Why did you not pick safer cage?"

"How in Qondyor's name was I to know? If you'd shaved your beard as I told you . . ."

"He can reach up! What do now?"

"Prepare to die like a man, I suppose," said Fallon, drawing his sword.

"But I have no weapon!"

"Unfortunate, what?"

The Krishnans in front of the cage yelled and screamed, though whether they were trying to distract the shan or were cheering it on to the assault Fallon could not tell. As for the shan, it ambled around to the section of the inclosure where the Earthmen were trapped and reared up against the rock so that its head came on a level with the men.

Fallon stood, ready to thrust as far as his limited footing allowed. The park keepers in front were shouting something at him, but he did not dare to take his eyes from the carnivore.

The jaws gaped and closed in. Fallon thrust at them. The shan clomped shut on the blade and, with a quick sideways jerk of its head tore the weapon from Fallon's hand and sent it spinning across the inclosure. The beast gave a terrific snarl. As it opened its jaws again, Fallon saw that the blade had wounded it slightly. Brown blood drooled from its lower jaw.

The monster drew back its head and gaped for a final lunge— and then a bucketful of liquid fell upon Fallon from above. As he blinked and sputtered, he heard Fredro beside him getting the same treatment, and became aware of a horrid stench, like that of the sheep-dip.

The shan, after jerking back its head in surprise, now thrust it forward again, gave a sniff, and dropped back down on all sixes with a disgusted snort. Then it walked back into its cave.

Fallon looked around. Behind and above him a couple of zoo keepers were holding a ladder against the outside of the fence at the point where Fallon and Fredro had scaled it. A third Krishnan had climbed the ladder and emptied the buckets of liquid upon the Earthmen below him. He was now handing the second bucket to one of his mates preparatory to climbing back down the ladder.

Another Krishnan, lower down the slope, called through the bars, "Hasten down, my masters, and we'll let ye out the gate. The smell will hold yon shan."

"What *is* the stuff?" asked Fallon, scrambling down.

"Aliyab-juice. The beast loathes the stench thereof, wherefore we sprinkle a trace of it upon our garments when we wish to enter its cage."

Fallon picked up his sword and hurried out the gate, which the keepers opened. He neither knew nor cared what aliyab-juice was, but he did think that his rescuers might have been a little less generous in their application of it. Fredro's bundle was soaked, and the Krishnan paper, which had little water-resistance, had begun to disintegrate.

A couple of the keepers closed in, hinting that a tip would be welcome as a reward for the rescue. Fallon, somewhat irked, felt like telling them to go to Hishkak, and that he was thinking of suing the city for letting him be chased into the cage in the first place. But that would be a foolish bluff, as Balhib had not yet attained that degree of civilization where a government allows a citizen to sue it. And they *had* saved his life.

"These blokes want some money," he said to Fredro. "Shall we make up a purse for them to divide?"

"I take care of this," said Fredro. "You are working for me, so I am responsible. Is matter of Polish honor."

He handed Fallon a whole fistful of gold pieces, telling him to give them to the head keeper to be divided evenly among those who took part in the rescue. Fallon, only too willing to allow the honor of the Polish Republic to meet the cost of rescue, did so. Then he said to Fredro, "Come along. We shall have to work hard to get all this stuff memorized."

Behind them, a furious dispute broke out among the keepers over the division of the money. The Earthmen boarded another omnibus and squeezed into the first seats they found.

For a while, the vehicle clattered westward along the northern part of the Bacha. Presently Fallon noticed that several seats around both Fredro and himself had become vacant. He moved over to where Fredro sat.

Across the aisle, a gaudily dressed Zanidu with a sword at his hip was sprinkling perfume on a handkerchief, which he then held to his nose, glaring at Fallon and Fredro over this improvised respirator. Another craned his neck to look back at the two Earthmen in a marked manner through a lorgnette. And finally a small spectacled fellow got up and spoke to the conductor.

The latter came forward, sniffed, and said to Fallon, "You must get off, Earthmen."

"Why?" said Fallon.

"Because you're making this omnibus untenable by your foul effluvium."

"What he say?" said Fredro, for the conductor had spoken too fast in the city dialect for the archeologist to follow.

"He says we're stinking up his bus and have to get off."

Fredro puffed. "Tell him I am Polish citizen! I am good as him, and I don't get off for . . ."

"Oh, for Qarar's sake stow it! Come along; we won't fight these beggars over your precious Polish citizenship." Fallon rose and held out a hand to the conductor, palm up.

"Wherefore?" said the conductor.

"You will kindly return our fares, my good man."

"But you have already come at least ten blocks . . ."

"Fastuk!" shouted Fallon, "I've had all the imposition from the city of Zanid today that I can put up with! Now will you . . ."

The conductor shrank back at this outburst and hastily handed over the money.

When they entered Fallon's house and disposed of their burdens, Fredro asked: "Where is your—ah—jagaini?"

"Away visiting," said Fallon brusquely, not caring to air his domestic upheavals at this stage.

"Most attractive female," said Fredro. "Maybe I have been on Krishna so long that greeny coloring looks natural. But she had much charm. I am sorry not to see her again."

"I'll tell her," said Fallon. "Let's lay out these robes and our clothes, and hope that most of the stench will disappear by the time we have to put them on again."

Fredro, unfolding the robes, sighed. "I have been widower thirty-four years. Have many descendants—children, grandchildren, and so on for six generation."

"I envy you, Dr. Fredro," said Fallon sincerely.

Fredro continued, "But no woman. Mr. Fallon, tell me, how does a Earthman go about getting the jagaini in Balhib?"

Fallon glanced at his companion with a sardonic little smile. "The same way you get a woman on Earth. You ask."

"I see. You understand, I only wish information as scientific datum."

"At your age you might, at that."

They spent the rest of the day rehearsing the ritual and practicing the gliding walk of the Yeshtite priest. For the third meal of the Krishnan day they went out to Savaich's.

Then they returned to Fallon's house. Fallon shaved off Fredro's whiskers, despite the latter's protests. A light dabbing of green face-powder gave their skins the correct chartreuse tinge. They gave their hair a green wash and glued to their heads the artificial ears and antennae that Mjipa had furnished.

Lastly they both donned the purple-black sacerdotal robes over their regular clothes. They left the hoods hanging down and hitched the skirts up to knee-length through the belt-cords. Then over these they put on each a Zanido rain-cloak—Fallon his new one and Fredro the old patched one that Fallon had been meaning to get rid of.

At last they set out for the Safq afoot. And soon the great enigmatic conical structure came into view against the darkening sky.

Chapter XIII

Fallon asked, "Are you sure you want to go ahead with this? It's not too late to back out, you know."

"Of course am sure. How—how many ways in?"

"Only one, so far as I know. There might be a tunnel over to the chapel, but that wouldn't do us any good. Now remember, we shall first walk past, to see in as far as we can. I think they have a desk beside the entrance, where one has to identify oneself. But these robes ought to get us in. We watch until nobody's looking, then nip around behind the bulletin-board and shed these rain-cloaks."

"I know, I know," said Fredro impatiently.

"Anybody'd think you couldn't wait to have your throat cut."

"When I think of secrets inside, waiting for me to discover them, I do not care."

Fallon snorted, giving Fredro the withering look that he reserved for foolhardy idealists.

Fredro continued, "You think I am damn fool, yes? Well Mr. Consul Mjipa told me about you. Said you were just like that about getting back that place you were king of."

Fallon privately admitted that there was justice in this comparison. But, as they were now entering the park surrounding the Safq, he did not have time to pursue that line of thought.

Fredro continued in a lower tone, "Krishna is archeologist's paradise. Is ruins and relics representing at least thirty or forty thousand Terran years of history—eight or ten times as long as recorded history on Earth—but all mixed up, with huge lacunae, and never properly studied by Krishnans themselves. A man can be a Schliemann, a Champollion, and a Carnarvon all at same time . . ."

"Hush, we're getting close."

The main entrance to the Safq was lit by fires, fluttering in the breeze, in a pair of cressets flanking the great doors. These doors now stood open. There was a coming and going of Krishnans, both priests and laymen, in and out of these doors. Voices murmured and purple-black robes flapped in the wind.

As Fallon and Fredro neared the entrance, the former could see over the heads of the Krishnans into the interior, lit by the light of many candles and oil-lamps. At intervals, the crowd would thin; and then Fallon could glimpse the desk at which sat the priest checking the register of those who entered.

Since the introduction of photography to Krishna, the priests of Yesht had taken to issuing to their trusted followers identification badges bearing small photographs of the wearers. Fifteen to twenty ingoing laymen stood in line, from the desk out through the doors and down the three stone steps to the street-level.

Fallon strolled up close to the portal, watching and listening. He was relieved to see that, as he had hoped, priests pushed through the traffic-jam in the portal without bothering to identify themselves to the one at the desk. Evidently for a layman to wear the costume of such a priest was so unheard-of, that no precautions had been taken against it.

Nobody heeded Fallon and his companion as they sauntered over to the bulletin-board and pretended to read it. A minute later, they popped out from behind the board, to all appearances third-grade priests of Yesht. The rain-cloaks lay rolled up on the paving in the shadow behind the board. The hoods of the robes shadowed their faces.

Fallon, heart pounding, strode towards the entrance. Laymen deferentially sidled out of his way so that he did not actually have to push through the crowd. Fredro followed so closely that he trod on Fallon's well-scuffed heels.

Through the scarred bronze valves of the great door they passed.

Ahead of them a partition wall jutted out from the left,

leaving only a narrow space between itself and the doorkeeper's desk on the right. On the left stood a couple of men in the armor of Civic Guards, leaning on halberds and scanning the faces of passers-by. A priest fluttered just ahead of Fallon, who heard him mutter something that sounded something like *"rukhval"* as he passed between the watchers on the left and the identification desk on the right.

Fallon lowered his head, hesitating before the plunge. Somewhere a bell tinkled. A whisper of movement ran through the crowd at the entrance. Fallon guessed that the bell meant to hurry up for the service.

He stepped forward, muttering *"Rukhval!"*, and feeling for the rapier-hilt under his robe.

The priest at the desk did not look up as Fallon and Fredro went past, being engrossed in a low-voiced colloquy with a layman. Fallon did not dare to look at the guards, lest even in the certain light they discern his Terran features. His heart stopped as a growl came from one of them: *"So'i! So'i hao!"*

So paralyzed was Fallon's brain with fear that it took a second to realize that the fellow was merely urging somebody to hurry up. Whether he was speaking to Fallon and Fredro, or to the priest and layman at the desk, Fallon did not wait to find out, but plunged on. Other priests crowded after the Earthmen.

Fallon let himself be carried along in the current. As he passed into the Safq he became aware of the curious sound that he had noticed when he had inspected the structure four nights before. It sounded more loudly inside than outside, but it also turned out to be a more complicated and more enigmatic noise than he had thought. Not only was there the deep rhythmic banging, but lighter and more rapid sounds as of hammering, plus grating noises as of filing or grinding.

The spate of Krishnans swept across the rear of the cella of the temple of Yesht that formed part of, or had been built into, the Safq, and that appeared as the large room in Kordaq's plan. Peering cautiously out from under the edge of his cowl to the left, Fallon could see the backs of the pews—three great blocks of them, about half filled. Beyond, as he passed behind the aisles dividing the pews, he glimpsed the railing that separated the congregation from the hierarchy. To the left of center rose the pulpit, a cylindrical structure of gleaming silver. At the rear of the center stood something black and uncertainly shaped. This would be the great statue of Yesht that Panjaku of Ghulinde, himself a Yeshtite, according to a story in the *Rashm,* had come to Zanid to make.

The lamplight glimmered on the gilding of the decorations and sparkled on the semi-precious stones set in the mosaics that ran around the upper parts of the walls. Fallon could not see these mosaics clearly from where he was, but he had an impression of a series of tableaux illustrating scenes from the myths of Yesht—a mythos notable even among the fanciful Krishnans for grotesquerie.

The stream of Krishnans coming in through the entrance sorted itself out in this space behind the rearmost pews. The laymen trickled forward into the aisles between the pews to find their places, while the priests, much fewer in number, pressed forward into another doorway straight ahead.

According to Liyara's instructions, Fallon surmised that through this door he would find a robing-room where the priests put on the over-vestments which they wore during the service. The lower grades, including the third, did not change their regular robes for this purpose. Only the highest grades, from the fifth up, donned complete special regalia.

With a glance back to make sure that Fredro was still following, Fallon plunged ahead through this door. But when he had passed through, he did not find himself in at all the sort of place that he expected from the nondescript little square that corresponded to this room on Kordaq's plan.

He was in a medium-sized room, poorly lit, with another door straight ahead, through which the priests ahead of him were hastening. And then the clink of a chain made him turn his head to the left. What he saw made him recoil so sharply as to step on the toe of the following Fredro, who squeaked.

Chained to the far wall of the room, but with plenty of slack to allow it to reach all parts of the chamber with its snaky neck, was a shan. While not so large as the ones that Fallon had seen in Kastambang's arena and the zoo, it was quite large enough to eat a man in a few mouthfuls.

At the moment the creature's head lay upon the forward pair of its six clawed feet. Its big eyes steadily regarded Fallon and his companion, not two meters away. One lunge would have caught either of them.

With a stifled gasp, Fallon pulled himself together and pressed forward, hoping that none of the Krishnans had observed his gaffe. He remembered the shower of aliyab-juice that he and Fredro had received earlier at the zoo. No doubt the shan would refrain from attacking them for this, if for no other reason. Could it be that all the priests sprinkled the stuff on their robes, so that any odorless intruders—disguised as Fallon and Fredro were—would be gobbled by the shan? Fallon could not tell whether the genuine priests smelled of aliyab because he had become habituated to it. But if this was true, their impromptu bath at the zoo had been fortunate.

The shan's eyes followed them, but the beast did not raise its head from its paws. Fallon hurried through the next door.

Ahead, the corridor extended in a long gentle curve following the outer wall of the building. There were no windows; and although jadeite is translucent in thin sections, the outer walls were much too thick to admit any outside light. Lamps were fastened at intervals to wall-brackets. The left side of the corridor was formed by another wall pierced by frequent doorways. Around the curve, where the bulge of the inner wall blocked more distant vistas, Fallon knew from the plan that there should be a flight of stairs leading up and another one down.

To the immediate left, there branched off a large hallway or elongated chamber crowded with priests shuffling about before a long counter, on which were piled the outer vestments. The priests were picking these up, donning them, and straightening them before a series of mirrors affixed to the opposite wall. Though there was a murmur of talk, Fallon noticed that the priests were unusually quiet for a crowd of Krishnans.

Having been briefed by Liyara, Fallon walked—with an air of confidence that he did not feel—down the counter until he came to a pile of the red capes which distinguished third-degree priests of Yesht. He picked up two, handed one to Fredro, and put on the other before one of the mirrors.

No sooner had he done so when a bell jangled twice. With last-minute scurrying and primping, the priests formed a double file along the side of the hall where the mirrors were hung. Fallon dragged Fredro, still fumbling with the tie-strings of his cape, into the first vacant space that he spotted in the double line of priests of the third class. These followed those of the fourth class, who wore blue capes, and preceded those of the second, who wore yellow. Fortunately there did not seem to be any fixed order in which those of a given class took their places.

Fallon and Fredro stood side by side, heads bowed to keep their faces hidden, when the bell rang three times. There was a shuffle of feet. Out of the corner of his eye, Fallon saw a heterogeneous group of Krishnans hurry by. One carried, swung from a chain, a thurible whence poured a cloud of fragrant smoke, the fragrance cutting through the pervasive aliyabstench and the strong Krishnan body-odor. There was one with a kind of harp and another with a small copper gong. There were several laden with gold-lace and jewels, carrying ornate staves with symbols of the cult on top.

And Fallon could not repress a start as a couple passed towing between them, by a metal collar to which chains were linked fore and aft, a naked female Krishnan with her wrists bound behind her back.

Though the light was uncertain, and Fredro did not get a good look, he thought that the female was one of the small paleskinned, short-tailed primitives from the great forest belt east of Katai-Jhogorai, beyond the Triple Seas. The westerly Krishnans had but a meager knowledge of these regions, save that the forest folk had long furnished the Varasto nations with most of their slaves. But most Krishnans were too proud, stubborn, and truculent to make good slaves. They were too likely to murder their masters, even at the cost of their own lives.

But the timid little forest people from Jaega and Aurus were still kidnapped for sale in the western ports of the Triple Seas, though this traffic had declined since the suppression of the pirates of the Sunqar.

Fallon had no time now to wonder what the Yeshtites meant to do with the forest-female. For the bell rang again, and the dignitaries sorted themselves out into a formal procession at the head of the column. The harpist and the gong-carrier began to make musical noises. The mass moved forward in a stately march that contrasted with their previous informal haste. As they marched, they broke into a wailing and lugubrious hymn. Fallon could not understand the words because the priests sang in Varastou—a dead language that was the parent of Balhibou, Gozashtandou, Qiribou, and the other tongues of the Varasto nations, who occupied the lands west of the Triple Seas.

Chapter XIV

Chanting dismally, the priests paraded down the robing-hall and through a door that opened into the side of the chapel. Led by the hierarchs and the musicians, they passed down the rightside aisle to the rear of the chapel, across the rear, and to the front again. Fallon's eyes swept over the decorations: rich and old and fantastically ornate, in which the safq-shell, as the principal symbol of the god, occurred over and over. Around the capital of one of the pillars a scaffolding showed where the priests were renewing some of the gilt.

Around the upper third of the walls ran the great mosaic illustrating the myth of Yesht. Fallon could interpret the pictures from Liyara's account. The god had been just an earthgod in the Varasto pantheon, having been adopted by the Varasto nations from the Kalwmians when they overran and broke up the latter's empire. In recent centuries, however, the priesthoods both of Yesht and of Bakh, the Varasto skygod, had developed henotheistic tendencies in Balhib, each trying to seize a monopoly of religion instead of living and letting live as in the old days of Balhibo polytheism. To date the Bakhites had had the better of the struggle, enlisting the dynasty among their worshippers and asserting that Yesht was no god at all but a horrid cacodaemon worshipped with obscene rites by the tailed races who had roamed the lands of the Triple Seas before the tailless Krishnans had settled the country many thousands of years before.

According to the current canonical myth of Yesht, the god had incarnated himself in a mortal man, Kharaj, in the days of the pre-Kalwm kingdom of Ruakh. In this form he had preached to the Krishnans.

Yesht-Kharaj overcame monsters and evil spirits, exorcized ghosts, and raised the dead. Some of his adventures seemed surrealistically meaningless to the outsider, but to the devotee no doubt had a profound symbolic significance.

At one time he was captured by a she-demon, and their offspring grew up to become the legendary King Myande the Execrable of Ruakh. After a long and intricate struggle between the god and his demidemoniac son, Yesht-Kharaj was arrested by the king's soldiers, tortured with great persistence and ingenuity, and at last allowed to die. The king's men buried the remains, but the next day a volcano burst from the ground at the spot and overwhelmed the king and his city.

The mosaic showed these events with exemplary candor and literalness. Fallon heard a low whistle from Fredro as the latter took in the tableau. Fallon trod on Fredro's toe to silence him.

The procession passed through a gate in the railing between the pews and the altar. There it split into groups. Fallon followed the other third-grade priests and squirmed into the rearmost rank of their section, hoping to be less conspicuous. He found himself on the left side of the altar as one faced it, with the cylindrical silver pulpit cutting off a good part of his view towards the congregation.

On his left, as he faced the audience, rose the great statue of Yesht, standing on four legs in the form of tree-trunks, wearing a mountain on his head and holding a city on one of his six outstretched hands and a forest on another. The remaining hands held other objects: one a sword, others things less easily identified.

Past the pulpit Fallon could see the altar between the statue and the congregation. He observed with some shock that the hierarchs were shackling the forest-female prone upon the altar by golden fetters attached to her wrists and ankles.

Beyond the altar, he now noticed, there stood a brawny Krishnan with his head concealed by a black cloth bag with eye holes. This Krishnan was setting up and heating an assortment of instruments whose purpose was obvious.

Fallon heard Fredro's appalled whisper: "Is going to be *tortures?*"

Fallon lifted his shoulders in a suggestion of a shrug. The chanting ceased and the most gaudily bedecked hierarch climbed the steps to the pulpit. From somewhere nearby Fallon heard a whisper in Balhibou, "What ails the third-grade section this Rite? They're so crowded one would think there was an extra man among 'em . . ."

Another whisper shushed the complainant, and the head hierarch began to speak.

The beginning of the service was not very different from those of some of the major Terran religions: prayers in Varastou; hymns, announcements, and so on. Fallon fidgeted, shifted his feet, and tried not to scratch. During the silences the little whimpering moans of the forest-female were heard. The hierarchs bowed to each other and to the statue, and handed symbolic objects back and forth.

Finally the chief hierarch ascended the pulpit again. The congregation became very quiet, so that Fallon felt that the climax was not far off.

The hierarch began in modern Balhibou: "Listen, my children, to the story of the god Yesht where he became a man. And watch, as we act out this tale, that you shall always be reminded of these sad events and shall carry the image of them engraven upon your liver.

"It was on the banks of the Zigros River that the god Yesht first came in unto and took possession of the body of the boy Kharaj as the latter played and sported with his companions. And when the spirit of Yesht had taken possession of the body of Kharaj, the body spake thus: 'O my playfellows, harken and obey. For I am no longer a boy, but a god, and I bring you word of the will of the gods . . .'"

During this narrative, the other hierarchs went through a pantomime illustrating the acts of Yesht-Kharaj. When the high-priest told how one of the boys had refused to accept the word of Yesht and mocked Kharaj, and the latter had pointed a finger at him and he fell dead, a gaudily clad priest fell down with a convincing thump.

The pantomime proceeded through the intimate details of the youth of Kharaj, with the unwilling assistance of the captive, who then played the role of the god as his gruesome death by torture was related. The eyes of the Krishnans—priest and layman alike—glistened at the spectacle. Fallon had to avert his, and beside him he heard Slavic mutterings from Fredro.

Anthony Fallon was not a man of high character. But though

he had been responsible for a certain amount of death and destruction on his own account in the course of his adventures, he was not wantonly cruel. He liked Krishnans on the whole —except for this sadistic streak which, though usually kept out of sight, came to the surface in such manifestations as this torture-sermon.

Now, though he tried to retain his attitude of cynical detachment, Fallon found himself grinding his teeth and driving his nails into his palms. He would cheerfully have blown up the Safq and everybody in it, as the obnoxious Wagner had suggested. Had Mjipa's missing Earthmen ended up on this bloody slab, too? Fallon, who did not much like the Bakhites either, had long discounted their accusations against the Yeshtites, attributing them to mere commercial rivalry. But now it transpired that the priests of Bakh had known whereof they spoke.

"Steady," he whispered to Fredro. "We're supposed to enjoy this."

The high priest called for another hymn, during which a collection was taken up. Then after prayers and benedictions the high priest came down the aisle from his pulpit and led the priests, chanting, down the aisle along the route that they had entered. When Fallon and Fredro, marching with the sacerdotal procession, passed back into the robing-hall, Fallon heard the general scurry of feet as the congregation departed out the main entrance, where the clink of coin told that another collection was being taken up. Watching the authentic priests, Fallon tossed his cape on the counter and strolled off with Fredro, still shaken by what he had witnessed.

The unexplained noises now came to Fallon's ears again more clearly, since there was no more singing and haranguing to drown them out. The other priests were either standing about in groups and talking, or drifting off about their own affairs. Fallon jerked his head toward the corridor that ran around the outer wall of the building.

Fallon and Fredro walked along this curving hallway. Above the level of the doorways on the left ran a series of inscriptions, at the sight of which Fredro became excited.

"Maybe in pre-Kalwm languages," he whispered. "Some of those I can decipher. Must stop to copy . . ."

"Not tonight you shan't!" hissed Fallon. "Can't you imagine what these blokes would think if they saw you doing that? If they caught us, they'd use us at the next Full Rite."

Some of the doors to the left were open, revealing the interiors of miscellaneous chambers used for storing records and transacting sacerdotal business. From one door came the smell of cookery.

Fallon could discern as he walked that the walls of the structure were of enormous thickness, so that the passages and rooms were more like burrows in a solid mass than compartments separated by partitions.

Nobody had yet stopped or spoken to the Earthmen as they rounded the gentle curve of the hall to the stair that Fallon was looking for. The noises came more loudly here. The stair took up only half the corridor; priests went up and down it.

Fallon walked briskly up the stair to the next level. This proved to be that on which the hierarchy had its living and sleeping quarters. The Earthmen snooped briefly about. In a recreation-room Fallon recognized the high priest, his gorgeous vestments replaced by a plain black robe, sitting in an armchair, smoking a big cigar and reading the sporting page of the *Rashm*. The mysterious noises seemed fainter on this storey.

Fallon led Fredro back down the stairs and started along the corridor again. Underneath the upgoing stair was the entrance to another stairway going down. At least so Fallon inferred, though he could not see through the massive iron door that closed the aperture. In front of this door stood a Krishnan in the uniform of a Civic Guard of Zanid; he held a halberd.

And Anthony Fallon recognized Girej, the Yeshtite whom he had arrested for brawling two nights previously.

Chapter XV

For three seconds, Fallon stared at the armed Krishnan. Then the gambler's instinct that had brought him such signal successes—and shattering failures—in the past prompted him to go up to the guard and say, "Hello there, Girej."

"Hail, reverend sir," said Girej with a questioning note in his voice.

Fallon raised his head so that his face was visible under the cowl. "I've come to collect on your promise."

Girej peered at Fallon's face and rubbed his chin. "I—I should know you, sir. Your face is familiar; I'll swear by the virility of Yesht that I've seen you, but . . ."

"Remember the Earthman who saved you from being run through by the Krishnan Scientist?"

"Oh! You mean you're really *not* . . ."

"Exactly. You won't give us away, will you?"

The guard looked troubled. "But how—what—this is sacrilege, sirs! 'Twould mean my . . ."

"Oh, come on! You don't mind playing a bit of a joke on those pompous hierarchs, do you?"

"A jest? In the holy temple?"

"Certainly. I've made a bet of a thousand karda that I could get into and out of the crypt of the Safq with a whole skin. Naturally I shall need some corroboration that I've done so—so there's one-tenth of that in it for you in return for your testifying that you saw me here."

"But . . ."

"But what? I'm not asking you to do anything irreligious. I'm not even offering you a bribe. Merely an honest fee for telling the truth when asked. What's wrong with that?"

"Well, good my sirs . . ." began Girej.

"And have you never wished to prick the pretensions of these conceited hierarchs? Even if Yesht is a great god, those who serve him are merely human like the rest of us, aren't they?"

"So I ween . . ."

"And didn't you promise me help when I needed it?"

This went on for some time; but few, Terran or Krishnan, could long resist Fallon's importunities when he chose to turn on the charm.

At last, when Fallon had raised the ante to a quarter of his winnings, the bewildered Girej gave in, saying, " 'Tis now near the end of the fourteenth hour, my masters. See that you return ere the end of the fifteenth, for at that time my watch does end. If you do not, you must needs wait until noon of the morrow, when I come on again."

"You stand ten-hour watches?" said Fallon, cocking a sympathetic eyebrow. As Krishnans divided their long day into twenty hours beginning at dawn (or, more accurately, halfway from midnight to noon) this would mean a watch of considerably more than twelve Terran hours.

"Nay," said Girej. "I have the night trick but once in five nights, trading back and forth with my mates. Tomorrow I'm on from the sixth through the tenth."

"We'll watch it," said Fallon.

The Krishnan leaned his halberd against the wall to open the door. This door, like many on Krishna, had a crude locking-mechanism consisting of a sliding bolt on both sides, and a large keyhole above each bolt, by means of which this bolt could be worked by a key thrust through from the other side. The bolt on the near side was in the home position, while that on the far side was withdrawn, and a large key stood idle in the keyhole giving access to the latter bolt.

Girej grasped the handle of the near bolt and snapped it back, then pulled on the fixed iron doorhandle. The door opened with a faint groan.

Fallon and Fredro slipped through. The door clanged shut behind them.

Fallon noticed that the mysterious sound now came much more loudly, as from a source just out of sight. He identified these sounds as those of a metal-works. He led his companion down the long dim-lit flight of stairs into the crypt, wondering if he would ever succeed in getting out.

Fredro mumbled, "What if he gives us away to priests?"

"I should like the answer to that one, too," said Fallon. "Luck's been with us so far."

"Maybe I should not have insisted on coming. Is bad place."

"A fine time to change your so-called mind! Straighten up and walk as if you owned the place, and we may get away with it." Fallon coughed as he got a lungful of the smoky atmosphere.

At the bottom of the stairs a passage of low-ceilinged, rough-hewn rock ran straight ahead, with openings on both sides into a congeries of chambers whence came the growing clangor. Besides the yellow glow of the oil-lamps in their wall-brackets, the labyrinth was fitfully lit by scarlet beams from forges and furnaces, the criss-crossing red rays giving an effect like that of a suburb of Hell.

Krishnans—mostly tailed Koloftuma of both sexes—moved through the murk, naked save for leather aprons, trundling carts of materials, carrying tools and buckets of water, and otherwise exerting themselves. Supervisors walked about.

Here and there stood an armed Krishnan in the gear of one of Kir's royal guard. Civic guards had replaced them only in the less sensitive posts. They shot keen looks at Fallon and Fredro, but did not stop them.

As the Earthmen walked down the corridor, a plan transpired out of the confusion about them. On the right were rooms in which iron ore was smelted down into pigs. These pigs were wheeled across a corridor to other rooms in which they were remelted and cast into smaller bars, which were turned over to smiths. The smith hammered the bars out into flat strips, beat them into rolls around iron mandrels, finally welded them into tubes.

As the Earthmen passed room after room, it became obvious what this establishment was up to. Fallon guessed the truth before they came to the chamber in which the parts were assembled. "Muskets!" he murmured. "Smoothbore muskets!"

He stopped at a rack, wherein a dozen or so of the firearms stood, and picked one out.

"How to shoot?" asked Fredro. "I see no trigger or lock."

"Here's a firing-pan. I suppose you could touch it off with a cigar-lighter. I knew this would happen sooner or later! It just missed happening when I tried to smuggle in machine-guns.

The I. C. will never put this cat back in the bag!"

Fredro said: "Do you think some Earthmen did this, having —ah—having got around hypnotic treatment, or that Krishnans invented them independently?"

Fallon shrugged and replaced the musket. "Heavy damned things. I don't know, but— I say, I think I can find out!"

They were standing in the assembly-room, where a couple of workmen were fitting carved wooden stocks to the barrels. On the other side of the room three Krishnans were conversing about some production problem: two men with the look of overseers, and one small elderly Krishnan with bushy jade-pale hair and a long gown of foreign cut.

Fallon strolled over toward these three, timing his approach to arrive just as the two foremen went their ways. He touched the sleeve of the long-haired one. "Well, Master Sainian," he said. "How did you get involved in this?"

The elderly Krishnan turned toward Fallon. "Aye, reverend sir? You queried me?"

Fallon remembered that Sainian was a little hard of hearing, and it would not do to shout private business at him in public. "To your private chamber, if you don't mind."

"Oh, aye. Hither, sirs."

The senior Krishnan led them through the tangle of rooms and passages to a section devoted to sleeping-accommodations: dormitories for the workers, crudely furnished with heaps of straw now occupied by snoring and odorous Koloftuma of the off shift—and individual rooms for officials.

Sainian led the Earthmen into one of the latter, furnished austerely but not uncomfortably. While there was no art or grace to this cubicle, a comfortable bed and armchair, a heap of books, and a plentiful supply of cigars and falat-wine were in evidence.

Fallon introduced the two savants in languages that each understood, then said to Fredro, "You won't be able to follow our conversation much, anyway. So if you don't mind, stand outside the door until we're finished, will you? Warn us if anybody starts to come in."

Fredro groused but went. Fallon closed the door and pushed back his hood, saying, "Know me now, eh?"

"Nay, sir, that I do not . . . but stay! Are you verily a Krishnan or a Terran? You look like one of the latter disguised as the former . . ."

"You're getting close. Remember Hershid, four years ago?"

"By the superagency of the universe!" cried Sainian. "You're that Earthman, Antane bad-Faln, sometime Dour of Zamba!"

"I say, not so loud!" said Fallon. Sainian, because of his infirmity, had a tendency to bellow an ordinary conversation.

"Well, what in the name of all the nonexistent devils do you here?" said Sainian in a lower voice. "Have you truly become a priest of Yesht? Never did you strike me as one who'd willingly submit to any cult's drug-dreams."

"I shall come to that. First, tell me: Are you down in this hole permanently, or can you come and go at will?"

"Ha! Then you cannot be an authentic priest, or you would know without the asking."

"Oh, I know you're clever. But answer my question."

"As to that," said Sainian, lighting a cigar and pushing the box toward Fallon, "I am as free as an aqebat—in one of the cages in King Kir's zoo. I come and go as I please—as does a tree in the royal gardens. In short, I roam this small kingdom of the cellar of the Safq without let or hindrance. But so much as a motion toward escape is worth a pike in my chaudron, or a bolt in my back."

"Do you like that state of affairs?"

" 'Tis a relative matter, sir. To say I like this gloomy crypt as well as the opulent court of Hershid were tampering with the truth. To say I mislike it as ill as being flayed and broiled like one of those wretches the Yeshtites employ in their major services were less than utter verity. Relativity, you see. As I have ever maintained, such terms as *'like'* are meaningless in any absolute sense. One must know what one likes better than . . ."

"Please!" Fallon, who knew his Krishnan, held up a hand. "Then I can count on you not to give me away?"

"Then it *is* some jape or masque, as I suspected! Fear not; your enterprises are nought to me, who tries to look upon the world with serene philosophical detachment. Albeit such traps as this wherein I presently find myself do betimes render difficult that worthy enterprise. Did a chance present itself of dropping demented Kir into some convenient cesspool, I think mundane resentment would overcome the loftiest . . ."

"Yes, yes. But how did you get caught?"

"First, good sir, tell me what do *you* do in this cursed mew? Not mere idle curiosity, I trust?"

"I'm after information. So . . ." Fallon, without going into the reason for wishing this information, briefly told of the methods by which he had penetrated the crypt.

"By Myande the Execrable! Hereafter I shall believe all tales I hear of the madness of Terrans. You had perhaps one chance in the hundred of getting this far without apprehension."

"Da'vi has stood by me this time," said Fallon.

"Whether she stands by you so staunchly on your way out is another matter whose outcome I eagerly await. I would not see your quivering body stretched upon the gruesome altar of Yesht."

"Why combine worship with torture? Just for fun?"

"Not entirely. There was once an ancient superstition in the land, that by periodically slaying a victim in such wise that the wretch was made copiously to weep, the heavens—by the principles of sympathetic magic—would likewise be induced to weep, thereby causing the crops to grow. And in time this grim usage attached itself to the worship of the earth-god Yesht. But the truth is, in very fact, that many folk like to see others hurt—a quality wherein, if I read my Terran history aright, we're not so different from you. Will you have a beaker of wine?"

"Just one—and don't tempt me with a second. If I have to fight my way out I shall need all my coordination. But let's have your story, now."

Sainian drew a deep breath and looked at the glowing end of his cigar. "Word came to me in Hershid that the Dour of Balhib was hiring the world's leading philosophers, at fabulous stipends, for a combined assault upon the mysteries of the universe. Being—like all men of intellect—somewhat of a fool in worldly affairs, I gave up my professorship in the Imperial Lyceum, journeyed to Zanid, and took service here.

"Now, mad though he be, Kir did have one shrewd idea—unless that cunning son-in-law of his, Chabarian, first put the burr in his drawers. Myself inclines to the Chabarian hypothesis, for the man once visited your Earth and picked up all sorts of exotic notions there. This particular idea was to collect such credulous lackwits as myself, clap us up in these caves, ply us with liquor and damsels, and then inform us that we should either devise a thing wherewith to vanquish the Qaathians or end up on the smoking altars of Yesht. Faced with this grim alternative, mightily have we striven, and after three years of sweat and swink we have done what no others on this planet have hitherto accomplished."

"And that was?" said Fallon.

"We have devised a workable gun. Not so handy and quick at vomiting forth its deadly pellets as those of Earth, but yet a beginning. We knew about Terran guns. And though none had ever seen one in fact, we sought information from those who had—such as the Zambava whom you led in your rash raid into Gozashtand back in the reign of King Eqrar. From this we ascertained the basic principles: the hollow metal tube, the ball, the charge of explosive and means for igniting it. The tube with its wooden stock presented no great difficulties, nor did the bullets.

"The crux of the matter was the explosive. We were chapfallen to find that the spore-powder of the yasuvar-plant, however lively in firecrackers and other pyrotechnics, was useless for our present purpose. After much experiment, the problem was solved by my colleague Nele-Jurdare of Katai-Jhogorai with a mixture of certain common substances. Thenceforth 'twas but a matter of cut-and-try."

"Stimulus-diffusion."

"What?"

"Never mind," said Fallon. "Just a Terran term I got from Fredro. Who was in on this project besides you?"

Sainian re-lit his cigar. "There were but two others worthy the name of philosopher: Nele-Jurdare—who, alas, perished in an accidental explosion of his mixture a while ago . . . . What date is it by the way? With nought to tell the time by but the changing of the guard, one loses track."

Fallon told him, adding, "Before I forget, three Earthmen—Soares, Botkin, and Daly—have disappeared from Zanid in the last three years. Have you seen any sign of them? They weren't included in Chabarian's ordnance department, were they?"

"Nay, the only other is my colleague, Zarrash bad-Rau of Majbur. The other leaders in this enterprise were but high-class mechanics, five of 'em, Krishnans all. Of these, three have died of natural causes. The other two remain on as supervisors till, if Kir keeps his promise, these tubes have proved their might upon the sanguinary field of battle, whereupon we shall be released with all the gold we can carry. Assuming, that is to say, the Dour does not cut our throats to silence us for certain, or that the Yeshtites do not track us down and slay us for knowing too much about their infernal cultus."

"Where's this Zarrash now?"

"He has the third chamber down. He and I are at the moment on terms of cold courtesy only."

"Why?" asked Fallon.

"Oh, a difference of opinion. A slight epistemological dissension, wherein Zarrash—as a realist-transcendentalist—upheld the claims of deductive reasoning. Now, I, as a nominalist-positivist was asserting those of inductive. Tempers rose, words flew—childish, I grant you, but long confinement frays the temper. But withal, in a few days we find ourselves driven to reconciliation by sheer tedium of having nobody else with whom intelligently to converse."

Fallon asked, "Do you know what the explosives are made of?"

"Oh, aye. But think not I will babble the news."

"You hope to sell that knowledge to some other Krishnan potentate—say the Dour of Gozashtand?"

Sainian smiled. "You may draw your own inferences, sir. I don't risk a straight answer before I am free of this trammel."

"What think you of the coming of the gun to this planet?"

"Well, the late Nele-Jurdare deplored the whole enterprise, assisting but unwillingly to preserve his own gore. He maintained that to further such murderous novelties were a sin against one's fellow being, unworthy of a true philosopher. Zarrash on t'other hand favors the gun on the ground it will end all war upon the planet, by making it too frightful for men to contemplate—for all that it had not that effect in Terran history."

"And you?"

"Oh, I look upon the matter from a different angle of vision: Until we Krishnans have some rough equality with you Terrans in force of arms, we cannot expect equality of treatment."

"Why, what's the matter with how you've been treated?"

"Nought is the matter, sir. Considering what you *could* have done, you've displayed exemplary moderation. But you're a variable and various lot. You have furnished us on one hand with Barnevelt—a paragon of manly virtue who has put down the Sunqar pirates and atop of that brought us the boom of soap. On the other hand, there have been palpable swindlers like that Borel. Your methods of selecting those who shall visit us baffle us. On one hand you stop your men of science from imparting their knowledge of useful arts to us—lest by taking advantage thereof we destroy your comfortable superiority. On the other hand, you unleash upon us a swarm of trouble-stirring missionaries and proselytizers for a hundred competing and contradictory religious sects, whose tenets are at least as absurd as those of our native cults."

Fallon opened his mouth to speak, but Sainian rattled on. "You are, as I have said, more variable than we. No two of you are alike, wherefore no sooner have we adapted ourselves to one of you when he is replaced by another of utterly different character. Take, for instance, when Masters Kennedy and Abreu—both credits to their species—retired at Novorecife and were replaced by those sottish barbarians Glumelin and Gorchakov. And your relations with us are at best those of a kindly and solicitous master to an inferior—who is not to be wantonly abused, but who will, if he knows what is well for him, bear himself in an acquiescent and deferential manner toward his natural lord. Take this consul at Zanid—what's his name . . ."

"I know Percy Mjipa," said Fallon. "But look here: Aren't you afraid your planet will get pretty badly shot up? Or that whoever gets guns first will conquer all the other nations?"

"For the first contingency, a man is no deader when slain by a gun-bullet than when clouted by a club. And for the second, that were no ill to my way of thought. We need one government for the world—first because we *must* have it ere you will admit us to your hoity-toity Interplanetary Council. Secondly, because it gives us an advantage in dealing with you in any case. Prestige follows power, she does not precede, as says Nehavend."

"But shouldn't such a government come about as a result of voluntary agreement among the nations?" Fallon smiled at the realization that he, the cynical adventurer, was arguing for Terran political idealism, while Sainian, the unworldly philosopher, spoke for Machiavellian realism.

"You'll never get voluntary agreement in our present stage of culture, and well you know it, Earthman. Why, if the ayamen of our nearest heavenly neighbor, the planet Qondyor—what do you Terrans call it?"

"Vishnu," said Fallon.

"I recall now—after some fribbling Terran deity, is it not? What I say is: if these rude savages invaded us—let's say brought hither in Terran spaceships for some recondite Terran reason—think you that even that threat would unite our several states? Nay. Gozashtand would seek revenge upon Mikardand for its defeat at Meozid. Suria and Dhaukia would see a chance to throw off the yoke of Qaath, and then each to erase the other—and so on down the list, each angling for the help of the invaders in extirpating its neighbor, indifferent to its own eventual fate.

"Had we another thousand years wherein to advance at our natural gait, 'twere well—but such time is lacking. And, as I recall my Terran history, you fellows all but blew up your planet before you came to that happy degree of concord; and your general level of culture was far ahead of our own at present. So, say I, we shall receive equal treatment when—and only when—we no longer have this multiplicity of independent sovereignties that you can play off, one against . . ."

"Excuse me," said Fallon, "but I've got to get back upstairs before my friend guarding the door goes off duty."

He crushed out his cigar, rose, and opened the door. There was no sign of Fredro.

"*Bakh!*" Fallon breathed. "Either the fool's gone off exploring on his own, or the guards have taken him! Come on, Sainian, show me around this warren, I must find my man."

Chapter XVI

Sainian led Fallon briskly through the halls and rooms of the crypt. Fallon followed, shooting glances right and left from under his cowl into the many dark corners.

Sainian explained: "Here the guns are stored when finished and inspected . . . Here is the room where the barrels are bored true after forging . . . Here is the stock-making chamber. See how they carve and polish stocks of bolkis-wood; Chabarian lured woodcarvers from Suruskand, for in this treeless land the art's but feebly developed . . . Here the explosive is mixed . . ."

"Wait," said Fallon, looking at the mixing process.

In the middle of the room a tailed Koloftu stood before a cauldron under which burned a small oil-flame. The cauldron contained what appeared to be molten asphalt. The Koloftu was measuring out with a dipper and pouring into the asphalt the materials from two barrels full of whitish powder, like fine sand, while with his other hand he gently stirred the mixture.

"Beware!" said Sainian. "Disturb him not, lest we all be blown to shreds!"

But Fallon stepped nearer to the cauldron, thrust a finger into one of the barrels of powder, and tasted. Sugar!

Though no chemist, Fallon's store of general information—gathered in the course of his ninety-four years—informed him that the other barrel probably contained niter. In back of the Koloftu, Fallon could see a mold into which the mixture would be poured to harden into small blocks. But he could not linger to watch this process.

They searched through more chambers: some used by the workers for living, some for storage of raw materials, and some vacant. In one section of the labyrinth, they came upon a door with a member of the Royal Guard standing before it.

"What's in there?" said Fallon.

" 'Tis the tunnel to the chapel across the street. In former times the priests used it for their convenience, especially in rainy weather. But now that the government has rented their crypt, they must needs slop through the wet like common mortals."

As they searched, Fallon started as a trumpet-call reverberated through the caverns. There was a bustle of guards clanking about, the lamplight gleaming on their armor.

"The guard is changed at midnight," said Sainian. "Be that a matter of moment to you?"

"Hishkak, yes!" said Fallon. "Now we can't leave until tomorrow noon. You'll have to put us up."

"What? But my dear colleague, it would mean my head were I caught harboring you . . ."

"It'll mean your head if we're caught, in any case, because you've been seen walking all over this place with me."

"Well then, it were not irrational for me to seek a boon from you in turn. Does that conspiratorial wit of yours hold some plan for freeing me from these noisome toils?"

"You mean you want to escape?"

"Certes!"

"But then you'll forfeit all this pay the government has supposedly been banking for you."

Sainian grinned and tapped his forehead. "My true fortune is in there. Promise to get me out—and Zarrash too if you can—and I'll hide you and your comrade. Though Zarrash be but an addlepated animist, yet I would not leave a professional colleague in such a lurch."

"I'll do my best. Oh, there's the *fastuk* now!"

Having scoured almost the entire cellar, they came upon Dr. Julian Fredro. The archeologist was standing before a section of ancient wall near the exit stairs on which appeared a faint set of inscriptions. In one hand he held a pad and in the other a pencil with which he was copying off the markings.

As Fallon approached with thunder on his face, Fredro looked up with a happy smile. "Look, Mr. F-Fallon! This looks like one of oldest parts of building, and the inscription may tell us when it was built . . ."

"Come along, you jackass!" snarled Fallon under his breath. On their way back toward Sainian's quarters, he told Fredro what he thought of him, with embellishments.

Sainian said, "There is room for but one here, so I will put the other in Zarrash's chamber." He tapped with his knuckle on Zarrash's door-gong.

"What is it?" asked another elderly Krishnan, opening the door a crack.

Sainian explained. Zarrash slammed his door shut, saying through the wood, "Begone, benighted materialistic chatterbox! Seek not to lure me into any such scheme temerarious. I have woes enough without harboring spies."

"But 'tis your chance to escape from the Safq!"

"*Ohe?* By Dashmok's paunch, that is an aya of a different gait." Zarrash reopened his door. "Come in, come in, ere you are overheard. What is that?"

Sainian explained in more detail, and Zarrash invited all to sit down to wine and cigars. Learning that Fredro was a Terran savant, both philosophers began to ply him with questions.

Sainian said, "Now, touching this matter of inductive versus deductive reasoning, dear colleague from Earth, perhaps you can with your maturer wisdom shed light upon our difference. What is your rede?"

Thus the conversation took off into the realms of higher reasoning, far into the night.

The following morning, Fallon felt the bristle upon his chin and looked at himself in Sainian's mirror. No Earthman could pass as a Krishnan with an incipient beard of the full European or white-race type. Krishnan whiskers were usually so sparse that the owners pulled them out, hair by hair, with tweezers.

Sainian slipped in, bringing a plate on which were the elements of a plain Krishnan breakfast.

"Be not palsied with fright," said the philosopher, "but the Yeshtites search their temple for a brace of infidels said to have attended last night's Rite, disguised in the habit of priests. The purpose of this intrusion and the identity of the intruders are not known. But since the doorkeepers swear that no such persons went out after the service, they must still be there. And they can't have descended into the crypt because the only door thereto is constantly guarded. I have no notion, of course, who these miscreants might be."

"How did they find out?"

"Some one counted the capes of the third-class priests and found that two more had been employed than there were priests to wear them. So, ere this mystery leads to wider searchings, methinks you and Master Yulian had best aroint yourselves ere you bring disaster upon us all."

Fallon shivered at the thought of the bloody altar. "How long before noon?"

"About an hour."

"We shall have to wait until then."

"Wait, then, but stir not forth. I'll do my proper tasks, and tell you when the guards have changed again."

Fallon spent the next hour in solitary apprehension.

Sainian put his head in the door, saying: "The guards have been changed."

Fallon pulled his hood well down over his face, glided out with the shuffling walk of the priests of Yesht, and gathered up Fredro in Zarrash's room. They headed for the exit stairway. The crypt was still lit by oil-lamps and the glow of furnaces, just as it had been before; there was no way to tell day from night. When Fredro sighted the carving that he'd been copying the night before, when Fallon had found him and dragged him off, he wanted to stop to complete his transcription.

"Do what you like," snarled Fallon. "I'm getting out."

He mounted the stairs, hearing Fredro's disgruntled shuffle behind him. At the top of the flight he came to the big iron door. With a final glance around, Fallon smote the door with his fist.

After a few seconds there was a clank as the outer bolt slid back, and the door creaked open. Fallon found himself facing a trooper of the Civic Guard in uniform—but not Girej. This Krishnan was a stranger.

Chapter XVII

For three seconds they stared at one another. Then the guard started to bring up his halberd, at the same time turning his head to call out, *"Ohe!* You there! I think these are the men for whom . . ."

At this instant Fallon kicked him expertly in the crotch, a form of attack to which Krishnans—despite many anatomical differences—are just as vulnerable as Earthmen. As the man yelled and doubled over, Fallon reached around the edge of the door and extracted the big key. Then he slammed the door and shot home the bolt on the stair side, so that those in the temple could not open it unless they either broke it down or found another key.

"What is?" said Fredro behind him.

Without bothering to explain, Fallon pocketed the key and trotted down the stairs. At such desperate moments he was at his best; as they reached the bottom there was a loud bang as something struck the door from the other side.

Fallon, calling upon his recollection of his tour of the crypt the previous night with Sainian, picked his way through the complex toward the tunnel entrance. Twice he went astray, but found his way again after scurrying about the passages like a rat in a psychologist's maze.

Behind him Fallon heard a scurry of feet on the stair and a clatter of weapons. Evidently the door had been opened.

At last he sighted the guard in front of the tunnel door. The Krishnan hoisted his halberd warily. Fallon kept right on, waving his arms and crying, "Run for your life! There's a fire in the explosives-room, and we shall all be blown to bits!"

Fallon had to repeat before the guard got the idea. Then the fellow's eyes goggled with horror; he dropped his halberd with a clatter and turned to unlock the door behind him.

The bolt had snicked back and the door was opening when Fallon, who had picked up the halberd, swung it so that the flat of the ax-head smote the guard on the helmet with a crashing *bong*. The man went down under the blow, half-stunned, and Fallon and Fredro slipped through the door.

Fallon started to shut the door, then realized that, first, the guard's body was lying in it; and second that if he did, the tunnel would be in total darkness. He could either leave it ajar, or drag the guard's body out of the way, take one of the lamps down from its bracket on the wall of the crypt, and close the door behind him.

The clatter of approaching footsteps convinced him that he would not have time to carry out this maneuver. So he took the key, leaving the door open, and turned into the tunnel, saying, "Now run!"

The two Earthmen gathered up the skirts of their robes and ran along the rough rock floor, sometimes stumbling on an irregularity. They ran, the light from the door behind them diminishing with distance.

"Be caref . . ."

Fallon started to speak, but ran headlong into another door in the darkness. He bumped his nose and cracked a knee-cap.

Cursing in several languages he felt around until he found the handle. When the door did not yield to mere pulling and pushing, he located the keyhole by feel and tried his two keys. One of them worked; the bolt on the far side slid back.

Noises from the other end of the tunnel indicated that their pursuers had found the felled guard.

"Hurry up, please!" whimpered Fredro between pants.

Fallon opened the door. They entered a room that was almost dark, but feebly lit by gleams of daylight that came down a stair-well. The walls were covered with shelves on which were untidily stacked vast numbers of books—Krishnan books with wooden covers and a long strip of paper folded zigzag between them. Fallon thought that he recognized them as the standard prayer-books of the cult of Yesht, but he had no time to investigate. The tunnel was echoing to the tramp of many running feet.

The Earthmen bounded up the stair, finding themselves on the ground floor of the Chapel of Yesht. Fallon, moving silently now, holding his scabbard through his robe lest it clank, neither saw nor heard any sign of life.

They went down a hallway, past rooms with rows of chairs set up in them, and presently found themselves in the vestibule just inside the front doors. The doors were bolted from inside, and Fallon slid back the bolt and opened one door.

A light rain slanted across the wet cobblestones and sprinkled Fallon's face. Few pedestrians were about. Fallon whispered,

"Come on! We'll slip out and around the corner to leave these robes. Then when the guards get here we shall be walking *toward* them."

Fallon slunk out the door and flitted down the stone steps and around the corner of the building into the narrow space between the chapel and the adjoining house. Here an ornamental shrub screened them from the street. They slipped off their robes, rolled them into small bundles, tied them up with their belt-cords, and tossed them into the top of the shrub where they were above eye-level and so might be overlooked. Then they walked quickly out to the street, turned, and were strolling past the front of the chapel when the door flew open again and a gaggle of guards and priests boiled out and clattered down the steps, peering into the rain, pointing, and shouting at one another.

Fallon, one fist on his hip and the other hand on his hilt, surveyed the pursuers with a lordly air as they came down the steps toward him. He gave them a little bow and a speech in his most grandiloquent Krishnan style, "Hail, good my sirs. May I venture to offer assistance in the worthy search upon which you appear to be so assiduously engaged?"

A guard panted at him: "Saw—saw you two men in the dress of priests of Yesht come out of yon portal even now?"

Fallon turned to Fredro with raised eyebrows. "Did we see anything like that?"

Fredro spread his hands and shrugged. Fallon said, "Though it grieves me so to confess, sir, neither my companion nor I noticed anything of the sort. But we've only just now arrived here—the fugitives might have left the building earlier."

"Well then . . ." began the Krishnan, but then another Krishnan who had bustled up during the colloquy said, "Hold, Yugach! Be not so ready to take the word of every passing stranger—especially inhuman alien creatures such as these. How know we they're not those for whom we seek?"

The other Krishnans, attracted by the argument, began crowding around with bared weapons. Fallon's heart sank into his soft-leather Krishnan boots. Fredro's mouth opened and closed in silence, like that of a fish in stale water.

"Who be ye, Earthmen?" said the first Krishnan.

"I'm Antane bad-Faln, of the Juru . . ."

The second Krishnan interrupted: *"Iya!* A thousand pardons, my masters—nay, a million, for not having known you. I was in the House of Justice when you testified against the robber Shave and his accomplice, the same which died of the wound ye so courageously dealt in apprehending him. Nay, Yugach, I'm wrong. This Antane's one of our staunchest trees of law and order. But come, sir, pray help us to search!"

The guard turned to shout directions to his fellows. For a quarter-hour Fallon and Fredro helped to hunt for themselves. At length, when the search appeared hopeless, the two Earthmen strolled off.

When they were out of earshot of the chapel, where the baffled searchers had gathered on the steps in a gesticulating knot, Fredro asked, "Is all over? I can go back to hotel now?"

"Absolutely. But when you write a report for that magazine of yours, don't mention me. And tell Percy Mjipa your story, saying we saw no trace of his missing Earthmen."

"I understand. Thank you, thank you, Mr. Fallon, for your help. A friend in need saves nine. Thank you, and good-bye!"

Fredro wrung Fallon's hand in both of his and looked around for a khizun to hail.

"You'll have to take a bus," said Fallon. "It's just like Earth. The minute a drop of rain falls all the cabs disappear."

He left Fredro and walked westward with the idea of going directly to Tashin's Inn to report to Qais, before events swept his news into obsolescence. He was getting wetter by the minute, and regretted the fine new rain-cloak lying by the front door of the Safq—he could almost see it from where he was. But he was not so foolhardy as to try to recover it now.

By the time he got to the Square of Qarar, however, he was limping from the knock that he had given his knee in the tunnel, and so wet and miserable that he decided to go home, get a drink, and change his clothes before proceeding farther. He had an old winter over-tunic there which he could use to keep dry with thereafter, and this would mean only a slight detour.

As he plodded through the rain, head down, the sound of a drum caused him to look around. Down Asada Street marched a column of civic guards with pikes on their shoulders, the drummer beating time at their head. From the two white bands on each sleeve of their jackets Fallon recognized them as belonging to the Gabanj Company. His own Juru Company looked scarecrows by comparison.

A few pedestrians lined the sides of the street to watch the column go past. Fallon asked a couple what the parade portended, but nobody could give him a plausible answer. When the militiamen had gone, Fallon trudged on homeward. He was just opening his door when a voice said, "Master Antane!"

It was Cisasa, the Osirian guardsman, with his antique helmet precariously held to the top of his reptilian head by the chin-strap and a Krishnan sword hanging awkwardly from a baldric over his shoulder, if he could be said to have a shoulder.

He went on in his weirdly accented Balhibou, "Fetch your

kear at once and come with me to the armory. The Churu Company is ortered out!"

"Why? Is the war on?"

"I know not—I do but pass on the orters."

Oh, Bakh! thought Fallon. *Why did this have to happen at this particular moment?* He said, "Very well, Cisasa. Run along and I'll be with you soon."

"Your parton, sir, but that I'm forpitten to do; I'm to escort you in person."

Fallon had hoped to slip away to continue his visit to Qais; but evidently Kordaq had foreseen that some of his guardsmen might try to make themselves scarce at mobilization, and had taken measures to forestall such absences. It was no use running away from Cisasa, who could outrun any Terran ever born.

Fallon's aversion to being called up was due, not to cowardice —he did not mind a good battle—but to fear that he would never, then, be able to collect from Qais.

He said wearily. "Come on in while I get my gear."

"Pray hasten, goot my sir, for I've three more to fetch after I've deliffered you. Have you no red jacket?"

"No, and I haven't had time to get one," said Fallon, rummaging for his field-boots. "Will you have a drink before we go?"

"No thank you. Duty first! I am wiltly excited. Are you not excited too?"

"Positively palpitating," grumbled Fallon.

The armory was crowded with the entire Juru Company, or at least all of those that had arrived; latecomers were being brought in every minute. Kordaq sat with his spectacles on at his desk, in front of which stood a line of guardsmen waiting to beg off from active service.

Kordaq heard each one out and decided quickly, usually against the plea for exemption. Those whose excuses he found frivolous he sent away with a stinging tirade on the cowardice of this generation compared to the heroic Balhibo ancestors. Those who claimed to be sick were given a quick examination by Qouran, the neighborhood physician, whose method seemed to be to count eyes, hands, and feet.

Fallon went over to where about two hundred of the new muskets were stacked against the wall. Other guardsmen were crowding around them, handling them and speculating as to how these things were to be used. He was turning one of the firearms over and sighting along the barrel—it had sights, he was glad to observe—when Kordaq's voice roared through the armory:

"Attention! Put those guns down and get back against the other wall, all of you, while in a few words I convey to you that which I must say."

Fallon, knowing the Krishnan habit of never using one word where ten would serve, braced himself for a long speech.

Kordaq continued, "As most of you know, the armies of barbarous Qaath have now swept across the sacred bourne of fair Balhib and are advancing upon Zanid. The holy duty therefore falls to us to smite them sore and hurl them back to regions whence they came. And here before you are the means, whereof I've hinted heretofore. These are true and veritable guns, such the mighty Terrans use, devised and fabricated here in Zanid secretly.

"If you wonder why the Juru Company, of all in Zanid the most irregulous, should be among the few chosen to bear this new weapon—for there are enough for three companies only—I'll tell you straight. Firstly 'tis known that our pike-drill's abominable and our archery worse, whereas those of some other companies of the Guards are almost up to the standards of the Regulars. 'Twere ill-advised, then, to deprive the army of such puissance as the pikes and bolts of these others provide. Secondly, the fact that this company includes beings from other planets—where such fearsome lethal toys are commonplace—makes us all the more adaptable. Thus these foreigners—I speak particularly of Earthmen and Osirians—can serve as a ready-made force of instructors in the use of guns.

"Did time permit, 'twould advantageous be to spend a number of days in practice—but the emergency o'errides our wishes. We must therefore march out at once and snatch such practice as we can enroute to the field of blood. Mark me well, though: there shall be no casual shooting without specific orders, for the quantity of bullets and explosive is limited. Do I catch any guard banging away unauthorized at stump and stone, I'll truss him and use him for a target at official exercise.

"Now for the manner whereby these things are used. Harsun, set up that bag of sand 'gainst yonder wall. Now attend me closely, heroes, whilst I strive in my inarticulate way to make these operations as clear as desert air."

Kordaq picked up a musket and proceeded to explain how it was loaded and fired. It transpired that, in the absence of any trigger mechanism, the musketeers were expected to discharge their pieces by touching to the firing-pans lighted cigars held in their teeth. Fallon had a prevision of some bloody noses before they learned to master the recoil of the guns.

One of the guardsmen said, "Well, meseems we get free smokes, at least."

Kordaq frowned at such levity and, having loaded his piece and lighted his cigar, aimed at the sandbag set up against the far wall and touched off his charge.

Bang!

The armory's rafters rang with the explosion. The kick of the musket staggered the captain, and from the muzzle bloomed a vast cloud of black, choking smoke. A hole appeared in the sandbag. Fallon, coughing with the rest, reflected that while the asphalt-sugar-niter mixture exploded, it might work better as smoke-screen material than as a propellant for ordnance.

The Krishnans in the company jumped violently. Several screamed with fright. Some shouted that they would be afraid to handle any such Dupulan's device as that. Others clamored for the good old pike and crossbow, which all understood. Kordaq quieted the hubbub and continued, emphasizing the importance of keeping one's explosive dry and one's barrel clean and oiled.

"Now," he said, "have you any queries?"

They had. The Thothians objected that they were too small to handle such heavy weapons, while the Osirians pointed out that tobacco-smoke threw them into a paroxysm of coughing, wherefore they never used the weed. Both arguments were allowed after much discussion, and it was decided that these species should retain their bills. After all, Kordaq told them, the company would need a few billmen to protect it, "lest for all our lightnings and thunders the roynish foe win to hand-play."

There remained the lone Isidian to dispose of—for while its elephantine trunk was efficient enough to catching thieves on the streets of Zanid, the creature was not quite up to manipulating a muzzle-loading arquebus. Fallon suggested making the Isidian the standard-bearer. Accepted.

The rain had ceased, and Roqir was breaking through the overcast, when the Juru Company marched out of the armory, with Captain Kordaq, the drummer, and the Isidian flag-bearer at their head, muskets and bills on their shoulders, and mailshirts clinking.

Chapter XVIII

The Balhibo army lay at Chos, a crossroads in western Balhib. Fallon, having the guard, walked slowly around the perimeter of the area assigned to the Civic Guard of Zanid, a musket on his shoulder. The Guard had the extreme northerly position in the encampment. Another regiment occupied the adjacent area, and another beyond that, and so on.

Krishnan military organization was much simpler than Terran, without the elaborate hierarchy of officers or the sharp distinction between officers and non-commissioned officers. Fallon was a squad-leader. Above him was Savaich, the tavern-keeper; as senior squad-leader of the section, he had limited powers over the whole section. Over Savaich was Captain Kordaq (the title of rank could be as well translated as "Major" or even "Lieutenant-Colonel") who commanded the Juru Company.

Above Kordaq was Lord Chindor who commanded the whole Guard; and above Chindor nobody but Minister Chabarian, who commanded the entire army. The army was theoretically organized in tens—ten-man squads, ten-squad sections or platoons, and so on. In practice, however, the numbers were seldom those of this theoretical desideratum. Thus the Juru Company, with a paper strength of a thousand plus, actually mustered less than two hundred on the battlefield, and it was about an average company. Staff work and supply and medical arrangements were of the simplest.

So far, Fallon and his squad had been adequately, if monotonously, fed. Fallon had not seen a map of the region in which they were travelling; but that mattered little because as far as one could see in all directions there was nothing but the gently rolling prairie with its waving cover of plants, something like Terran grasses in appearance, though biologically more like long-stemmed mosses.

From over the horizon a thin pencil of black smoke slanted up into the turquoise sky, where Ghuur's raiders had burned a village. Such cavalry-raids had struck deep into Balhib already. But the Qaathians could not take the walled cities with cavalry alone, nor could they build siege-engines on the spot, in a land where the only trees were grown from seeds imported and planted and kept alive by frequent watering.

All this Fallon either knew from rumors that he had picked up or surmised from his previous military experience. Now to his ears came the creak of supply-wagons, the animal noises of cavalry mounts, the hammering of smiths repairing things, the shrill cries of a tribe of the Gypsy-like Gavehona who had attached themselves to the army as camp-followers, the popping of muskets, as Kordaq doled out the day's sparing allowance of target powder and shot. In the six days since they had left Zanid, the Juru Company had acquired a nodding acquaintance with their new weapons. Most of them could now hit a man-sized target at twenty paces.

So far, there had been two killed and five wounded—four gravely—in musket accidents. One's gun had blown up, as a result either of faulty manufacture or of double-charging. The other had been shot on the target-range by a musketeer who failed to notice where he was pointing his piece. All seven casualties had occurred among the Krishnans of the company. The non-Krishnans were more careful, or more accustomed to firearms.

A spot of dust appeared above the prairie, about where the westward road would be. It grew, and out of it appeared a rider loping along on an aya, having the misfortune to have his dust-cloud blown along by the breeze at just his own speed. Fallon saw the fellow gallop into the camp and disappear from sight among the tents. This happened often enough, though sooner or later, he knew, the arrival would bear portentous news.

Well, this seemed to be the occasion, for a trumpet blew, riders galloped hither and yon, and Fallon saw the musketeers come marching back over the rise to camp. He, too, walked over to where the Juru Company's standard rose amid the tents. The troopers of the company were whetting swords, polishing helmets, and pushing oiled rags into their musket-barrels.

Just as Fallon arrived, the little drummer—a short-tailed freedman from the forest of Jaega—beat "fall in." With much clatter and last-minute rummaging for gear, the company slowly pulled itself together. Fallon was almost the first of the third section to arrive in his place.

At last they were all in place—except a couple. Cursing, Kordaq sent Cisasa over to the tents of the Gavehona.

Meanwhile a troop of cavalry galloped westward along the road trailing a rope, to the end of which was attached a rocket-glider, for Chabarian had hired a number of these primitive aircraft and their pilots from Sotaspe for scouting. The craft rose like a kite. When the pilot found an updraft, he cast off the rope and ignited the first of his rockets which, burning the spores of the yasuvar-plant, pushed the craft along.

Then the Juru Company stood and stood. Cisasa returned with the missing men. Krishnans on ayas galloped back and forth bearing messages. Officers, their gilded armor blinding in the bright sun, conferred out of earshot of the troops. Two of the companies of the Zanid Guard were wheeled out of line and marched across the front of the army to reinforce the left wing.

Fallon, leaning boredly on his musket, reflected that things had been different when he had commanded an army and so had had a fair notion of what was happening. He had, so to speak, started at the top and worked his way down in military rank. If he ever again acquired an army of his own, he would try to keep his soldiers better informed.

About him the men yawned, fidgeted, and gossiped: " 'Tis said the Kamuran has a kind of mechanical bishtar, worked by machinery and sheathed in iron armor . . ." "They say the Jungava have a fleet of flying galley-ships which, fanning the air with oars like wings, will hover over us and lapidate us with weighty stones . . ." "I hear Minister Chabarian has been beheaded for treason!"

Finally, more than an hour after falling in, there came a great blaring of trumpets and banging of gongs and beating of drums, and the army began to move forward. Fallon, tramping through the long moss-grass with the rest, saw that the commanders were getting the array into the shape of a huge crescent with the horns, of which the Zanid Guard was the right-hand tip, pointing westward toward the enemy. The musketeers had been massed at the tips of the crescent, with the more conventional units of pikemen and crossbowmen in between, while behind the crescent Chabarian had placed his cavalry. He had a squadron of bishtars, but kept them well back, for these elephantine beasts were too temperamental to be used rashly, and were prone to stampede back through their own army.

When they had marched so that the tents were mere dots against the eastern horizon they halted and stood again, while the officers straightened out irregularities in the line. There was nothing for Fallon to see except the waving of the moss-grass in the breeze and a glider circling overhead in the greenish-blue sky against the bright-yellow disk of Roqir.

The Juru Company was moved a little to place it atop a rise. Now one could see farther, but all there was to see was the surface of the olive-green plain, rippling like water as the breeze bowed the moss-grass. Fallon guessed the total force as in the neighborhood of thirty thousand.

Now he could see the road, along which more dust-clouds appeared. This time whole squadrons of riders were moving along it. Others popped up above the horizon, like little black dots. Fallon inferred from their behavior that they were Balhibo scouts retreating before the advance of the Jungava.

Then more waiting; then more Balhibo riders. And quite suddenly, a pair of riders a few hundred paces away were circling and fighting, their swords flashing like needles in the sun. Fallon could not see clearly what happened, but one fell off his mount and the other galloped away, so the Balhibu must have lost the duel.

And finally the horizon crawled with dots that slowly grew into squadrons of the steppe-dwellers spread out across the plain.

Kordaq said, "Juru Company! Load your pieces! Light your cigars!"

But then the enemy stopped and seemed to be milling around

with no clear purpose. A group of them detached themselves from the rest and galloped in a wide sweep that took them past the Juru Company, yelping and loosing arrows as they went, but from such a distance that nearly all the shafts fell short. One glanced with a sharp metallic sound from the helmet of a trooper, but without harm. Fallon could not see them too clearly.

From the left end of the line came a single report of a musket and a cloud of smoke.

"Fool!" cried Kordaq. "Hold your fire, hold your fire!"

Then with a tremendous racket the Qaathian army got into forward motion again. Fallon had a glimpse of a phalanx of spearmen marching down the road toward the center of the Balhibo line, where Kir's royal guard was posted. The phalanx was no doubt composed of Surians, or Dhaukians, or some other ally, as the Qaathian force was said to be entirely mounted. Other forces, mounted and afoot, could be seen moving hither and thither. Clouds of arrows and bolts filled the intervening air, the snap of the bowstrings and the whizz of the missiles providing a kind of orchestral accompaniment to the rising din of battle.

But the scene became too obscured by dust for Fallon to make much of it from where he stood, besides which the Juru Company would soon have its hands full with its own battle.

A huge force of mounted archers on ayas thundered toward the right tip of the crescent. Kordaq cried, "Are you all loaded, lit, and ready? Prepare to fire. Front rank, kneel!"

The first two ranks raised their muskets, the men of the second aiming over the heads of the first. At the end of the line Kordaq sat on his aya with his sword on high.

Arrows began to swish past. A couple thudded into targets. The approaching cavalry was close enough for Fallon, aiming his musket like the rest, to see the antennae sprouting from their foreheads when Kordaq shrieked "Give fire!" and lowered his sword.

The muskets went off in a long ragged volley that completely hid the view in front of the company behind a vast pall of stinking brownish smoke. Fallon heard cries beyond the smoke.

Then the breeze wafted the smoke back over the company and the atmosphere cleared. The great mass of aya-archers was streaming off to the right around the end of the line. Fallon saw several ayas kicking in the moss-grass before the company, and a couple more running with empty saddles. But he could not count the total casualties because the moss-grass hid the fallen riders.

"Third and fourth ranks, step up!" shouted Kordaq.

The third and fourth ranks squeezed forward between the men in front of them, who retired to reload.

From somewhere to the south came the sound of another volley of musketry as the left end of the line let go in its turn, but Fallon could see nothing. Behind the company rose a furious din. Looking back he saw that a large part of the mounted archers had swept around behind the Balhibo foot, but here had been set upon by one of the bodies of Balhibo cavalry. Kordaq ordered the Osirians and Thothians, who were standing in clumps behind the line of musketeers and leaning on their bills, to form a decent line to protect the company from an attack in the rear.

Meanwhile, another force appeared in front of the Juru Company; this was mounted on the tall shomals (beasts something like humpless camels) and carrying long lances. As they galloped forward the leading ranks again brought up their pieces. Again the crackling volley and the cloud of smoke; and when the smoke had cleared, the shomal-riders were nowhere to be seen.

Then nobody bothered the Juru Company for a time. The middle of the Balhibo line was hidden in dust and sent up a terrific din as spearmen and archers locked in close combat swayed back and forth over the bodies of the slain and hewed and thrust at one another; the plain shook with charges and countercharges of cavalry.

Fallon hoped that Prince Chabarian knew more about what was going on than he did.

Then Kordaq called his company to attention again as a mass of hostile pikemen materialized out of the dust-clouds, coming for the Zaniduma at a run. The first musketry volley shook the oncoming spearmen, but the pressure of those behind kept the mass moving forward. The second volley tore great holes in their front rank, but still they came on.

The first two ranks of musketeers were still back loading; the guns of the others had just been emptied. Kordaq ordered the bills forward, and the Osirians and Thothians squeezed through the ranks to the front.

"Charge!" shouted Kordaq.

The Osirians and Thothians advanced down the slope. Behind them the musketeers dropped their muskets, drew their swords, and followed. The sight of all the non-Krishnans seemed to unnerve the pikemen, for they ran off, dropping their pikes and yelling that devils and monsters were after them.

Kordaq called his company back to the hilltop, riding around in circles like an agitated sheep-dog and beating with the flat of his sword those of his men who showed a disposition to chase the enemy clear back to Qaath.

They re-formed on the hilltop, picking up and reloading their muskets. The sight of the corpses that now littered the gentle slope before them seemed to have heartened them.

The day wore on. Kordaq sent an Osirian to fetch water. The company beat off three more cavalry charges from different directions. Fallon surmised that they did not have to hit any opponents to accomplish that; the noise and smoke alone would stampede the ayas and shomals. For a while, the fighting in the center seemed to have died down. Then its pace quickened.

Fallon said, "Captain, what's the disturbance down toward the center?"

"They've been disturbed ever since the first onset . . . But hold—something's toward! Meseems men of our coat do flee back along the road to home. What can it be, that having so stoutly withstood the shock and struggle so long, they've now turned faint of liver?"

A mounted messenger came up and conferred with Lord Chindor, who cantered over to Kordaq, shouting, "Take your gunners across the rear of our host to the center of the line, and speedily! The Jungava have disclosed a strange, portentous thing! This messenger shall guide you!"

Kordaq formed up his company and led them in a quick march out behind the lines and southward across the rear. Here and there were clusters of wounded Krishnans, on whom the army's handful of surgeons worked as they could get around to them. To the Juru Company's right stood the units of balestiers and pikemen, battered and thinned—the greenish tinge of the Krishnans' skins hidden under a caking of dust down which drops of sweat eroded serpentine channels. They leaned upon their weapons and panted, or sat on convenient corpses. The moss-grass was trampled flat and stained purplish-brown.

Toward the middle of the line, the noise and dust began to rise again. The soldiers in the line were crowding to look over each other's shoulders toward something out of sight. Then the crossbowmen were shooting into the murk.

"This way," said the messenger, wheeling his aya and pointing to a gap in the line.

Kordaq on his aya, the drummer, and the Isidian standard bearer led the company through the line and deployed them to face the foe. At once Fallon saw the "thing."

It looked like a huge wooden box, the size of a large tent, and it rolled forward slowly on six large wheels, which were however almost entirely hidden by the thick qong-wood sides. On top was a superstructure with a hole in front; and behind the superstructure rose a short length of pipe. As the contraption crept forward at a slow walk, the pipe puffed clouds of mixed smoke and steam—puff-puff-puff-puff.

"By God," said Fallon, "they've got a *tank!*"

"What said you, Master Antane?" asked the Krishnan next to him, and Fallon realized that he had spoken in English.

"Merely a prayer to my Terran deities," he said. "Hurry up—straighten out the line."

"Prepare to fire!" shouted Kordaq.

The tank puff-puffed on, closer and closer. It was not headed for the Juru Company, but for a point in the Balhibo line south of it. Its qong-wood sides bristled with arrows and bolts stuck in the hard wood. Behind it crowded a mass of hostile soldiery. And now, out of the dust, another tank could be seen, farther down the line.

A loud *thump* came from the nearest tank. An iron ball whizzed from the aperture at the front of the superstructure and into the midst of the block of pikemen facing it. There was a stir in the mass. Pikes toppled and men screamed. The whole mass started to flow formlessly back from the line.

The muskets of the Juru Company crashed, spattering the side of the tank with balls. When the smoke had blown away, however, Fallon saw that the tank had not been materially damaged. There was a grinding of gears and the thing backed up a few feet, turning as it did so, and started forward again, continuing to turn until it pointed right toward the company.

"Another volley!" screamed Kordaq.

But then the *thump* came again, and the iron ball streaked in amongst the Juru Company. It struck Kordaq's aya in the chest, hurling the beast over backwards and sending the captain flying. Then, rebounding, the ball struck the Isidian in the head and killed the eight-legged standard-bearer. The standard fell.

Fallon got in one well-aimed shot at the aperture on the tank, and then looked around to see his company breaking up, crying: "All's lost!" "We're fordone!" "Every wight for himself!"

A few more shots were fired wildly, and the Juru Company streamed back through the gap in its own lines. The tank swung its nose toward the line of Balhibo pikemen again.

Thump! Down went more pikes. And Fallon, as he ran with the rest, had a glimpse of a third tank.

Then he was running in a vast disorganized mass of fugitives—musketeers, pikemen, and crossbowmen all mixed in together, while after them poured the hordes of the invaders. He stumbled over bodies and saw on both sides of him mounted Qaathians ride past him into the mass, hacking right and left with their scimitars. He dropped the musket, for he was practically out of powder and shot; and with the collapse of the Balhibo army he would have no chance to replenish his supply. Here and there, groups of Balhibo cavalry held together and skirmished with the steppe-folk, but the infantry were hopelessly broken.

The press thinned out somewhat as the faster runners drew ahead of the slower and the pursuers tore into the fugitives. Behind and above Fallon's right shoulder a voice shouted in Qaathian. Fallon looked around and saw one of the fur-hatted fellows sitting on an aya and brandishing a scimitar. Fallon could not understand the sentence but caught the questioning inflection and the words "Qaath" and "Balhib." Evidently the Qaathian was not sure which army Fallon, lacking a proper uniform, belonged to.

"Three cheers for London!" cried Fallon, and caught the Qaathian's booted leg and heaved. Out of the saddle went the Krishnan, to land on his fur hat, and into it went Anthony Fallon. He turned his mount's head northward, at right angles to the general direction of rout and pursuit, and kicked the beast to a gallop.

Chapter XIX

Four days later, having detoured around the battle zone to the north, Fallon reached Zanid. The Geklan Gate was jammed with Krishnans struggling to get in: runaway soldiers from the Battle of Chos, and country folk seeking the city as a refuge.

The guards at the gate asked Fallon his name and added several searching questions to make him prove himself a true Zanidu even though a non-Krishnan.

"The Juru Company, eh?" said one of them. " 'Tis said ye all but won the battle single-handed, hurling back hordes of the steppe-dwellers with the missiles from your guns when they sought to roll up your army's flank, until the accursed steam-chariots of the foe at long last drave ye from the field."

"That's a more truthful description of the battle than I expected to hear," replied Fallon.

" 'Tis just like the treacherous barbarians to use so unfair a weapon, against all the principles of civilized warfare."

Fallon refrained from saying that if the Balhibuma had won, the Qaathians would be making the same complaint about the guns. "What else do you know? Is there any Balhibo army left?"

The second guard made the Krishnan equivalent of a shrug.

" 'Tis said Chabarian rallied his cavalry and fought a skirmish at Malmaj, but was himself there slain. Know ye aught of where the invaders be? Ever since yester-morn folk have come through babbling that the Jungava are hard upon their heels."

"I don't know," said Fallon. "I came by the northern route and haven't seen them. Now may I go?"

"Aye—when ye've complied with one slight formality. Swear ye allegiance to the Lord Protector of the Kingdom of Balhib, the high and mighty Pandr, Chindor er-Qinan?"

"Eh? What's all this?"

The guard explained, "Well, Chabarian fell at Malmaj, as ye know. And my lord Chindor, arriving in haste and yet bloody from the battlefield, went to convey the news of these multiple disasters to his Altitude, the Dour Kir. And whilst he was closeted with the Dour, the latter—taken by a fit of melancholy—plucked a dagger from his girdle and slew himself. Then Chindor prevailed upon the surviving officers of the Government to invest him with extraordinary powers to cope with this emergency. So swear ye?"

"Oh, yes, of course," said Fallon. "I swear."

Privately, Fallon suspected that Kir's departure from the world of the living had been hastened by Chindor himself, who might also have coerced the other ministers at sword's point to accede to his dictatorship.

Passed by the guard, he rode at a reckless speed through the narrow streets to his own house. He feared that his landlord might have moved new tenants in, as his rent was in arrears. But he was pleased to find the little house just as he had left it.

His one objective now was to collect the other two pieces of Qais' draft, by fair means or foul. Then he'd go to Kastambang's and collect the remaining third of the draft, perhaps with a plausible story of Qais' having given him the paper in token of his indebtedness before fleeing the city.

Fallon hastily washed up, changed his clothes, and stuffed such of his belongings as he did not wish to abandon into a duffel bag. A few minutes later he went out, locked his door—for the last time, if his plans worked—strapped the bag to the aya's back behind the saddle, and mounted.

The gatekeeper at Tashin's Inn said that yes, indeed, Master Turanj was in his quarters, and the good my lord should go right up. Fallon crossed the court, now strangely deserted by Tashin's histrionic clientele, and went up to Qais' room.

Nobody answered his stroke on the door-gong. He pushed the door, which opened to his touch. When he looked in, his hand flew to his hilt, then came away.

Qais of Babaal lay sprawled across the floor, his jacket stained with brown Krishnan blood. Fallon turned the corpse over and saw that the spy had been neatly run through, presumably with a rapier. His script lay on the floor beside him amid a litter of papers.

Squatting upon his haunches, Fallon went through these papers. Not finding the slip that he sought, he searched both Qais' body and the rest of the room.

Still no draft. His first foreboding had been correct: Somebody who knew about the trisected draft had murdered Qais to get it.

But who? As far as Fallon could remember, nobody knew about this monetary instrument save Qais, Kastambang, and himself. The banker had custody of the money; if he wished to embezzle it, he could do so without written instruments to authorize him.

Fallon went over the room again, but found neither the piece of the draft nor clues to the identity of Qais' slayer.

At last he gave up, sighed, and went out. He asked the gatekeeper: "Has anybody else been in to see Turanj recently?"

The fellow thought. "Aye, sir, now that ye call it to mind. About an hour or more ago one did visit him."

"Who? What was he like?"

"He was an Earthman like yourself, and like ye clad in civilized clothes."

"But what did he *look* like? Tall or short? Fat or thin?"

The gatekeeper made a helpless gesture. "That I couldn't tell ye, sir. After all, all Earthmen look alike, do ye not?"

Fallon mounted his aya and set out at a brisk trot to eastward, across the city to Kastambang's bank. This trip might well prove a sleeveless errand, but he could not afford to pass up even the slightest chance of getting his money.

A subdued excitement ran through the streets of Zanid. Here and there Fallon saw a pedestrian running. One man shouted, "The Jungava are in sight! To the walls!"

Fallon rode on. He passed the House of Judgment, where the execution-board seemed to have more than its normal quota of heads. He did not look at the gruesome tokens closely, but as his eye swept down the line he was struck by the feeling that one of them was familiar.

Jerking his gaze back, he was horrified to observe that the fleshy head in question, its jowls hanging slack in death, was that of the very Krishnan whom he was on his way to see. The board under the head read:

KASTAMBANG ER-'AMIRUT,
    Banker of the Gabanj,

Aged 103 years 4 months.
Convicted of treason
on the tenth of Harau.
Executed on the twelfth instant.

The treason in question could be nothing but Kastambang's banking for Qais of Babaal, knowing the latter as an agent for Ghuur. And since torture of convicted felons—to make them divulge the names of their confederates—was a recognized part of Balhibo legal procedure, Kastambang in his final agonies might well have mentioned Anthony Fallon. Now Fallon had a reason for getting out of Zanid even more pressing than the prospect of the city's being surrounded and stormed by the Qaathians.

Fallon speeded up to a canter, determined to dash out the Lummish Gate and leave Zanid behind him without more delay. But after he had ridden several blocks, he realized that he was passing Kastambang's counting-house, which lay directly on his route to the gate. As he passed, he could not help noticing that the gates of the bank had been torn from their hinges.

Overpowering curiosity led him to pull up and turn his aya into the courtyard. Everywhere were signs of mob depredations. The graceful statues from Katai-Jhogorai littered the pave in fragments. The fountains were silent. Other objects lay about. Fallon dismounted and bent to examine them. They were notes, drafts, account-books, and the other paraphernalia of banking.

Fallon guessed that after Kastambang had been arrested, a mob had gathered and, on the pretext that a traitor's goods were fair game, had sacked the place.

There was just a chance that at least one of the thirds of Qais' drafts might be found here. He really should not, Fallon thought, take the time to search for it, with Zanid such a hot spot. But it might be his final chance to recover Zamba.

And what about the mysterious murderer of Qais? Had this character preceded Fallon here to Kastambang's?

Fallon went around the courtyard, examining every scrap of paper. Nothing there.

He passed on in, finding the battered corpse of one of Kastambang's Kolofto servants sprawled just inside the main door.

Now where would these fragments of the draft most likely be? Well, Kastambang had stowed his third in the drawer of that big table in his underground conference-room. Fallon resolved that he would search that room; and if he failed to find the paper there, he would leave the city forthwith.

The elevator was, of course, not running, but he found a stairway that led down to the lower level. He took a lamp from a wall-bracket, filled its reservoir from another lamp and trimmed the wick, and lit it with his pocket-lighter. Then he descended the stairs.

The passage was dark except for that one lamp. His footsteps and breath sounded loud in the silence.

Fallon's "bump of direction" carried him through the sequence of doors and chambers to Kastambang's "lair." The portcullis had not even been lowered. A couple of coins that the mob had dropped winked up from the floor; but the door to the lair itself was closed.

Now why? If the mob had stormed in and out, they would not likely have taken the trouble to close doors behind them.

The door was not quite closed, but ajar, and a thread of light showed under it. Hand on hilt, Fallon put a foot against the door and pushed. The door swung open.

The room was lit by a candle in the hands of a Krishnan woman, who stood with her back to the door. Facing Fallon on the other side of the conference-table stood an Earthman. As the door opened the woman spun around. The man whipped out a sword.

The *wheep* caused Fallon to snatch out his own blade as a matter of reflex, though when he got it out he stood holding it, his mouth gaping with astonishment. The woman was Gazi er-Doukh and the man was Welcome Wagner, in Krishnan costume.

"Hello, Gazi," said Fallon. "Is this another jagain? You're changing them fast nowadays."

"Nay, Antane—methinks he does indeed have the true religion, that for which I've long sought."

As Gazi spoke, Fallon took in the fact that the huge table had been assaulted with axe and chisel until it was a mere ruin of its splendid self. The drawers had all been hacked or forced open and the papers that had lain in them were scattered about the floor. In front of Wagner on the scarred surface lay two small rectangular slips of paper. Though Fallon could not read them from where he stood, he was sure from their size and shape that they were the fragments that he sought.

He said to Wagner, "Where'd you get those?"

"One from the guy that had it, and the other outa this drawer," said Wagner. "Sure took me long enough to find it, too."

"Well, they're mine. I'll take them, if you don't mind."

Wagner picked up the two slips with his left hand and pocketed them. "That's where you're wrong, mister. These don't belong to nobody—so if there's any money in it, it'll go to the True Church where it belongs, to help spread the light. I suppose you got the other piece."

"Hand those over," said Fallon, moving nearer.

"You hand yours over," said Wagner, stepping out from behind the table. "I don't aim to hurt you none, Jack, but Ecumenical Monotheism needs that dough a lot worser'n you do."

Fallon took another step. "You killed Qais, didn't you?"

"It was him or me. Now do like I say. Remember, I used to be pretty hot with these stickers before I seen the truth."

"How did you find out about him?"

"I went to Kastambang's trial and heard the testimony. Gazi knowed about the check being tore in three parts, so I put two and two together."

"Cease this mammering!" said Gazi, setting down her candle on the table. "You can divide the gold, or fight your battle elsewhere. But with the city on the edge of falling we've no time for private wannion."

"Always my practical little sweetheart," said Fallon, and then to Wagner again: "A fine holy man you are! You intend to murder two men and run off with the loot and the lady, all in the name of your god . . ."

"You don't understand these things," said Wagner mildly. "I ain't doing nothing immoral like you did. Gazi and me are gonna have strictly spiritual relations. She'll be my sister . . ."

At that instant Wagner leaped catlike, his rapier shooting out ahead of him. Fallon parried just in time to save his life; Wagner stopped his riposte-double with ease. The blades flickered and gleamed in the dimness, *swish-zing-clank!*

The space was too confined for fancy footwork, and Fallon found himself hampered by the lamp in his left hand. His exertions scattered drops of oil about. Wagner's arm was strong, and his swordplay fast and adroit.

Fallon had just made up his mind to throw the lamp into Wagner's taut, fanatic face when Gazi, crying: "Desist, lackwits!" caught his tunic from behind with both hands and pulled. Fallon's foot slipped on some pieces of paper. Wagner lunged.

Fallon saw the missionary's point coming toward his midriff. His parry was still forming when the point disappeared from his view, and an icy pain shot through his body.

Wagner withdrew his blade and stepped back, still on guard. Fallon heard, above the roaring in his ears, the clang as his own sword fell to the stone floor from his limp hand. His knees buckled under him and he slid to the floor in a heap.

Dimly he was aware of his lamp's striking the floor and going out; of an exclamation from Gazi, though what it meant he could not tell; of Wagner's fumbling through his scrip for the fragment of the draft; and lastly of the retreating footsteps of

Wagner and Gazi. Then everything was dark and quiet.

Fallon was never sure whether he had lost consciousness or not, and if so for how long. But an indefinite time later, finding himself asprawl on the floor in the dark with his tunic soaked with blood and his wound hurting like fury, it seemed to him that this would be a rotten place to die.

He began crawling toward the door. Even in his present condition, he did not mistake the direction. He dragged himself a few meters before exhaustion stopped him.

A while later he crawled a few meters more. He made a fumbling effort to feel his own pulse, but failed to find it.

Another rest, another crawl. And another, and another. He was getting weaker and weaker, so that each crawl was shorter.

Hours later, it seemed, he found the foot of the stair down which he had come. Now, could he even consider crawling up all those steps, when it was all he could do to pull himself along horizontally?

Well, he would not live any longer for not trying.

Chapter XX

Anthony Fallon came to in a clean bed in a strange room. As his vision cleared he recognized Dr. Nung.

"Better now?" asked Nung, who then did to him all the things that physicians do to patients to determine their state of health. Fallon learned that he was in the consul's house. Some time later, the doctor went out and came back with two Earthmen, Percy Mjipa and a leathery-looking white man.

Mjipa said, "Fallon, this is Adam Daly, one of my missing Earthmen. I got them all back."

After acknowledging the introduction in his ghost of a voice, Fallon asked, "What happened? How did I get here?"

"The Kamuran saw you lying in the gutter in the course of his triumphal procession up to the royal palace and told his flunkeys to toss you out with the other offal. Lucky for you, I happened along. As it was, you were within minutes of going out for good by the time I got you here. Nung just pulled you through."

"The Qaathians took Zanid?"

"Surrender on conditions. I arranged the conditions, mainly by convincing Ghuur that the Zaniduma would fight to the death otherwise, and by threatening to stand in front of the Geklan Gate myself while he tried to knock it down with a battering-ram. These natives respect firmness when they see it, you know, and Ghuur's not such a fool as to court trouble with Novorecife. I'm not supposed to interfere, but I didn't care to see Ghuur's barbarians ruin a perfectly good city."

"What were the conditions?"

"Oh, Balhib to retain local autonomy under Chindor as Pandr—a treacherous swine, but there didn't seem any alternative. And no more than two thousand Qaathians to be let into the city at once, to discourage robbery and abuse of the Zaniduma."

"Could you hold Ghuur to that, once he got the gates open?"

"He lived up to it. His record of keeping his word is better than that of most of these native headmen. And besides, I think he was a little afraid of me. You see he'd never seen an Earthman with my skin-color, and the superstitious beggar probably thought I was some sort of demon."

"I see," murmured Fallon. He understood one thing now: that quaint as some of Mjipa's affectations of superiority to the "natives" might be, they had the partial justification that Percy Mjipa was, as an individual, a superior sort of Earthman.

"How about the missing Earthmen?"

"Oh, that. Ghuur's men had carried them off—another coup arranged by your late friend Qais. The Kamuran has a hideout in Madhiq where he makes arms."

"But they've been pseudo-hypnotized . . ."

"Yes, and un-pseudo-hypnotized as well. Seems there's a Krishnan psychologist who studied at Vienna many years ago, before the technological blockade was tightened up, and he had worked out a method of undoing the Saint-Remy treatment. He worked his stunt on these three, and—you tell it, Mr. Daly."

Adam Daly cleared his throat. "When we'd had the treatment the Kamuran came to us and told us to invent something to beat Balhibuma, or else. There was no use pretending we couldn't, or didn't know how, and so forth. He even had another Earthman—some fellow we never heard of—hauled in and his head chopped off in front of us just to show us he wasn't fooling.

"We thought of guns, of course, but none of us could mix gunpowder. But we did know enough practical engineering to make a passable reciprocating steam-engine, especially as the Kamuran had a surprisingly fine machine-shop set up for us. So we built a tank, armored with qong-wood planks and armed with a fixed catapult. The first couple didn't work, but the third was good enough to serve as a pilot model for mass production.

"The Kamuran ordered twenty-five of the things and pushed the project with all his power; but what with shortages of metals and things, only seventeen of them were actually started—and what with breakdowns and bugs only three arrived at the battle. And from what I hear of the musketry of the Balhibo army, I take it that Balhib had been doing something similar."

"Yes," said Fallon, "but that was an all-Krishnan project. "Good-bye technological blockade. And I see the day when the sword will be as useless here as on Earth, and all the time I spent learning to fence will be wasted. By the way, Percy, what happened to the Safq?"

Mjipa replied, "Under the treaty, Ghuur has control of all armament facilities, so when the priests of Yesht closed their doors on his men he had 'em pile the Balhibo army's remaining store of powder against the doors and blew 'em in."

"Did the Qaathians find a couple of Krishnan philosophers named Sainian and Zarrash in the crypt?"

"I believe they did."

"Where are they now?"

"I don't know. I suppose Ghuur has them in confinement while he decides what to do with them."

"Well, try to get 'em free, will you? I promised I'd try to help 'em."

"I'll see what I can do," said Mjipa.

"And where's that ass Fredro?"

"He's happy, photographing and making rubbings in the Safq. I persuaded Chindor to give him the run of the place after Liyara the Brazer—for reasons you can guess—prevailed upon the Protector to suppress the cult of Yesht. Fredro's babbling with excitement—says he's already proved that Myande the Execrable was not only a historical character but built the Safq as a monument to his father—who wasn't Kharaj but some other chap. Kharaj, it seems, was centuries earlier, and the myths mixed them all up. And Myande was called the Execrable not because of anything he did to his old man, but because he beggared his kingdom and ran all his subjects ragged building the thing . . . But if you're interested he'll be glad to tell you himself."

Fallon sighed. "Percy, you seem able to fix up everything for everybody, except getting me back my kingdom." He turned to Daly. "You know, those tanks of yours wouldn't have been worth a brass arzu against anybody who knew about them ahead of time. They could easily have been ditched, or overturned, or set afire."

"I know, but the Balhibuma didn't," said Daly.

Fallon turned back to Mjipa. "How about Gazi and Wagner and those people? And my friend Kordaq?"

Mjipa frowned in thought. "As far as I know, Captain Kordaq never came back from Chos—so he's either dead, or a slave in Qaath. Gazi's living with Fredro."

Fallon grinned wryly. "Why, the old . . ."

"I know. He took an apartment—said he'd probably be here

for a year or more, so . . . Dismal Dan Wagner, you'll be pleased to hear, tried to lower himself down the city wall by a rope one night and was shot by a Qaathian archer."

"Fatally?"

"Yes. It seems he'd been trying to reach Majbur to cash a draft from the late Qais on Kastambang's bank, not knowing that the Balhibo government sent orders by the last train from Zanid to the Majbur bank to sequester Kastambang's account, he being a convicted traitor."

"Unh," said Fallon.

Dr. Nung appeared, saying: "You must go now, gentlemen. The patient has to rest."

"Very well," said Mjipa, rising. "Oh, one more thing. As soon as you're well enough to travel, we shall have to smuggle you out of the city. The Zaniduma know you spied for Ghuur. They can't arrest and try you openly, but a lot of them have sworn to assassinate you at the first opportunity."

"Thanks," said Fallon without enthusiasm.

A Krishnan year later, a disreputable-looking Earthman slouched along the streets of Mishe, the capital of Mikardand. His eyes were bloodshot, his face bore a stubble of beard, and his gait was unsteady.

He had peddled a small item of gossip to Mishe's newspaper, the oldest of Krishna. He had drunk half the proceeds and was on his way with the remainder to the dismal room that he shared with a Mikardando woman. As he staggered along, Anthony Fallon muttered. The passing Knight of Qarar who turned to stare did not understand the words, not knowing English.

" 'F I can only work one deal—one good old coup—I'll get an army, and I'll take that ruddy army to Zamba, and I'll be king again . . . Yesh, *king!*"